THE MERCHANT'S MANSION

BRAD DUNNE

THE MERCHANT'S MANSION

BRAD DUNNE

ENGEN
BOOKS

Published in Canada by Engen Books, St. John's, NL.

Library and Archives Canada Information is available on their website.

ISBN-13: 978-1-77478-092-3

Distributed by:
Engen Books
www.engenbooks.com
submissions@engenbooks.com

First mass market paperback printing: March 2022

Cover Design: Ellen Curtis
Cover Photo: Liz LeDrew Photography

This book is dedicated to Mom
My biggest fan

CHAPTER ONE

Nick opened his eyes and saw Charlotte staring back at him anxiously.

"The lights are on," she said.

Rising from sleep, he struggled to understand what she was talking about.

"Uhh?" he answered.

"The lights are on," she repeated.

"Did you leave them on before you came to bed?"

"No."

"Maybe you turned them on when you went to the bathroom."

"I think someone's in the house."

Nick groaned.

"Can you just go check for me, please?" she asked.

He got out of their full-sized bed, which took up most of the room, and saw that the light above the staircase was on. The bathroom and spare room were both dark. Before walking downstairs, he listened for footsteps around the apartment. After about a minute of silence, he walked down the steps. The kitchen light was on, and he saw the oven ticker read 3:33 am. Through the slits of the blinds, he could see night was still onyx black with no sign of dawn. He turned on the light in the living room, illuminating the small couch, coffee table, and laptop they used as a television, then did a quick sweep of their small apartment and was satisfied there was no one here. After making sure the door and windows were locked, he went to the fridge and drank a mouthful of milk straight from the carton. Charlotte would've given him hell, but he figured he'd earned it after this little bit of late-night/early-morning nonsense. As he put the milk back, he noticed the pungent smell of salt water, of the ocean. It reminded him of the times his dad used to drag him out to the beach for capelin or kelp for the garden. He could almost hear his dad's voice telling him the stench was "the pride of his country." But where was the smell coming from? The kitchen was clean, and nothing had been left out. Besides, he didn't even have anything like that in his fridge or freezer. Maybe it was the couple in the adjacent apartment who had a habit of missing garbage day, letting all kinds of odours accumulate. He went back upstairs, turning off the remaining lights.

"What took you so long?" Charlotte asked.

"I was being thorough."

"What do you think caused it?"

"I dunno. I'm too tired to think about it."

She lay flat on her back, her body tense. Nick wrapped his arms around her and rubbed her stomach until he felt her relax. The night had softened to a deep purple and they soon fell asleep for another couple hours. When they got up and came downstairs to make breakfast, Nick noticed the stink was gone.

"Did you notice a fishy smell last night before bed?" he asked her. The pot of water on the stove began to boil. He swirled it gently then dropped a cracked egg into it.

"No," she replied, slicing up an avocado. "Why? I don't smell anything now?"

"No reason. I thought I smelled it last night when I came down. It's not a big deal."

"My parents used to boil saltfish all the time, and it would stink out the house. Kids made fun of me because sometimes I'd come to school reeking like cod. I had to put all my clothes in the closet to keep the smell out. Now I can't stand it. Does that make me a bad Newfoundlander?"

Nick grinned and handed her a browned slice of toast with avocado and poached egg.

"By the way," Charlotte continued, looking at her phone. "I Googled sleepwalking, and apparently stress and anxiety can cause it."

Nick sat down with her and plunged the French press, pushing down on the coarse grinds. "Are you saying I got up and turned on all the lights last night because I'm stressed out?"

Charlotte shrugged. "Maybe. You've definitely got a lot on your mind lately. Between your dad and your job."

You mean my lack of job, Nick thought to himself. And lack of dad, really.

"I should drive out to see mom today," he said. "It's been almost a week since I last seen her. That might put my mind at ease."

Charlotte took the French press and poured them both

mugs of coffee. Nick took his black, savouring the astringent flavour. Charlotte set her coffee down and stared at it with both hands wrapped around the mug, watching the milk swirl. He knew something was on her mind.

"I've felt a presence in the house lately," she said.

Here we go, he thought but didn't speak aloud. He waited for her to continue.

"I don't think it's malevolent, but it wants something," she explained.

"What could a 'presence' want with us?" Nick asked.

Charlotte shrugged and drank her coffee.

"I've never understood your thing with the paranormal. You're a scientist. You have a legit job as a lab instructor. Seems contradictory to me."

"Not really. Being a scientist means observing phenomena with an open mind, taking in the empirical data before reaching a conclusion. I'm just trying to have an open mind, that's all."

Nick left it at that.

After breakfast, they dressed and dragged themselves into Nick's ten-year-old Toyota. The coffee had only managed to soften the sluggishness he felt from his disrupted sleep. He drove her to Memorial University's science building where she worked. She gave him a quick kiss goodbye before she got out of the car. An ugly bubble of jealousy swelled in his belly as he watched her trot away. He had worked at the university, too, at the Writing Centre before the oil tanked and funding was slashed. Charlotte had managed to survive the cuts. God forbid the bean counters go after STEM. Fortunately, their rent was cheap enough that they could get by on just her earnings, but his

EI was up now, and he felt increasing pressure to secure some kind of decent job. But with Newfoundland's tanking petrocurrency, he'd have better odds going off into the woods hunting a unicorn.

He pulled out of the university's parking lot towards Tim Hortons for an XL before getting onto the highway. It wasn't fair to feel resentful towards Charlotte. He needed to push his mind somewhere else. NOFX had a new album out that he'd been looking forward to listening to. He connected his phone to a radio adapter plugged into the car's cigarette lighter then cranked the music until the plastic inside the old Corolla vibrated with the kick drum. The music's tempo drove his foot deeper into the gas pedal as he weaved around traffic, making his way out of St. John's metastasizing sprawl. But as the monotonous kilometres of the Trans-Canada Highway clicked by, he couldn't resist the tidal drag of his mind's fixations. Whenever he felt stressed lately about finding a job, he dwelled on the time he'd wasted between high school and when he'd first enrolled in university at the age of twenty-one. He used to tell himself this had been an advantage, that it gave him some of the maturity needed to excel like he had. Finishing an honours degree followed by a Master of Arts in five years was pretty respectable, but he couldn't help but brood about those three years between eighteen and twenty-one when all he cared about was getting fucked up and playing shows with his band. Those three years could have been spent more productively, which would have made him less fragile in this economy. Deeper than that, he regretted the stress he put his parents through. Doubly, if he were in a better professional situation, he'd be able to support them like his sister did. But it wasn't his fault his biological parents had been neglectful drug addicts and... He took a deep breath and turned off the music. His mind was drifting into dangerous water. He switched over to a podcast on Roman history, something that would better hold his attention. NOFX hadn't released a good album in about ten years anyway.

The highway ended and spat him out at Carbonear—the only town in the Avalon peninsula outside the metro region big enough to warrant a Walmart—and from there it was all outports, little communities nestled into Newfoundland's crenellated shore. Nick enjoyed this part of the drive. The country road snaked along the coastline, sprinkled with balkanized townlets of about two dozen people, along with a few abandoned saltbox houses. A gentle snowfall dappled forgotten root cellars, their empty doorframes looking out onto the road like the open eye sockets of hollowed out skulls.

Cachot Cove, which the locals pronounced "catch-it," was right at the tip of the Baccalieu Trail, a two-hour drive from St. John's. The road dipped sharply downwards through a hallway of blasted purple rock, like descending through the stone gates into the underworld, before entering the southside of Cachot Cove then rising again in the northside. Spread out like a bow tie, the town's 100 or so houses were divided between the Catholic side to the south and the Protestant north. In the middle, the harbour lay dormant with the fish plant closed for the season and the small fleet of boats tied to the wharf. His was the only car occupying the slim streets, weaving through sleepy houses and properties scattered across the cove.

The merchant's mansion presided over Cachot Cove from the top of the northside. Nick envisioned its previous owner, Alistair Moore, keeping an eye on the harbour from the top of the two-storey centre bay window like the Tower of Sauron. Or at least that's how he imagined it used to look back in its glory days. Now it was more like an old, blind cyclops. His parents had gotten the chimney and roof re-done and up to code, but the house still needed a lot of work done before it could pass as a bed and breakfast.

He pulled into the driveway. Behind the Moore property was a private copse, a rare patch of trees amidst the denuded landscape devoid of topsoil, now covered by a thin blanket of snow. Nick didn't like how quiet it was. No birds or squirrels seemed to live there. A silent darkness rimmed by scraggly branches repelled any and all comers. There was a single crow sitting on a fence post with one eye on the house and one on the road, as if ready to flee at any moment should the house try to reach out and grab it. The rest of its murder cawed at it from a telephone wire, daring it to go closer, like a bunch of schoolboys playing a game. A sudden breeze shook the copse. The crow lost its nerve and took flight back to the telephone wire.

Nick knocked on the door and entered. As per usual, the house was nearly as cold inside as it was outside. The white elephant was a nuisance to heat, especially during winter. His dad hadn't gotten the chance to properly insulate the place. Heat rose up through the staircase and vanished.

"Nick?" his mother called out. "Is that you?" She was in the kitchen.

"Yup!" Nick answered.

"I wish you'd called. I could have got some lunch ready for you, too."

"You never answer it anyway. Is it even charged?"

She had to think about that. "I'm not sure."

Nick turned to the living room, which had been converted to his father's nursing unit.

"You can go in and sit with him while I finish getting his lunch ready," she offered.

Fred was bundled up in bed watching television. A low sour smell pervaded the room, which made Nick flinch whenever he entered. Fred looked at Nick with pale blue eyes, staring through him into some fathomless middle distance. His eyes, which had once shone with an electric blue intensity, appeared ghostly and preternatural, almost glowing. Just a few months ago, despite not being able to speak, Nick could detect a sense of recognition in his father's eyes whenever he visited. Now even that was gone. Every now and then he'd smack his stomach for some reason unknown likely even to himself. But mostly, he'd just stare.

The television was set to CBC news. They were talking about the price of oil and whether it was ever going to go back to the way it was. Consensus seemed to be likely not. Nick changed it over to Sportsnet. At least the Raptors were playing well.

Olivia joined them with a bowl of lukewarm soup. Nick sat up and let her sit beside Fred; she insisted on feeding him. It was strange to Nick that despite being seemingly immune to everything around him, his dad still opened his mouth to accept a spoonful of soup. When

Olivia raised a spoonful to Fred's mouth, he'd pop his lips open like an obedient child would. And whenever a bit dribbled down his chin, she dutifully wiped it away. The instinct to receive and consume food must be a function of the mind buried deep in the brain. However, that too would eventually go once the dementia mercifully reached its endgame.

After lunch was over, Olivia left then came back with two large bowls of water, one sudsy and one clear. Nick stripped away his father's blankets and Olivia tore off his old diaper, which reeked like stale piss. They did all of this without speaking. Olivia started with her husband's face and hair, rinsing out the towel in the bowl of clear water. She worked her way down to his arms, chest, and stomach. Fred's legs were mottled pink and purple from rheumatoid arthritis. It reminded Nick of someone with the early stages of frostbite. Before his fall in the shower, Fred could get around just fine, but during his long stay in the hospital his legs degraded like bananas left out in the sun. His mom should've just left him in the hospital at that point, which would've saved everyone a lot of misery, but she'd convinced herself she could nurse him back to health. It was delusional. But his mother was stubborn and wouldn't be talked out of it. Now she was up to her ears with her nearly catatonic husband and a B&B project that was only half finished. What a state.

After his legs and feet were done, Nick grabbed his dad's wrists and hauled him over so his mom could get at his back, the vertebrae sticking out like a stegosaurus. Fred's forearms, once thick and roped with sinewy muscle, were brittle twigs in Nick's hands. He thought of the times he'd watch his father drive a nail through a chunk of 2x4 with just two strikes of the hammer. Olivia finished by washing her husband's undercarriage with a fresh cloth and replaced his pull-up. Nick found a spot on the wall to examine during this final stage.

Olivia looked beyond tired, beyond exhausted. Nick guessed she'd lost about fifty pounds in the last six months. Her hair was thinning—he could see portions of her pale scalp—and her eyes were swollen with puffy bags. More than that, she started to remind Nick of his dad: forgetting things, seeming out of it, talking in long circular ramblings, forgetting whatever point she was trying to make. This was called "caregiver's dementia." The demanding work, stress, and lack of sleep caused the caregiver to experience similar symptoms as the person they were trying to take care of. Nick didn't have to be a psychiatrist to see she was burned out. Worrying about where this was leading gave him a sinking feeling in his gut.

"Any luck on jobs?" she asked.

"Nothing yet," he replied.

"Are you following up?"

"Yes," he lied. Not like that sort of thing worked anyway. His mom liked to lecture him about the job market despite the fact she'd only had two different teaching positions her entire life. The first in Stephenville, where she met his dad, and the second in St. John's, where she worked for thirty years.

"You should start studying for the LSAT while you're off work. I always said you'd be a great lawyer. Dad thought so, too."

Nick nodded, knowing full well he wasn't going to do

any such thing.

"You know what your problem is, don't you?" she asked.

Nick braced himself.

"It's those bloody tattoos. Any employer sees you coming in with those, they know right off the bat they're not going to hire you."

He had to admit she might be right about that. He'd started covering himself with ink as soon as he turned eighteen and didn't need his parents' permission. It wasn't like any of it was offensive, but if he had his time back, he probably wouldn't have gotten his hands and neck done.

"Have you heard back from the social worker?" he asked.

Olivia huffed and rolled her eyes then gave Nick a hard look. She knew that he'd just performed a brilliant chess move by pivoting the conversation away from him and towards something she couldn't resist talking about.

"A month ago, she told me she was going to put in his application for long term care, which she said takes about a week to process. So, two weeks go by, and I call her asking about an update. Turns out she didn't file it properly and had to do it over again."

Nick sighed. "Then I guess she should've heard by now?"

"Maybe. I don't want to call her. I feel like I'm being a nuisance. She said once it's filed it shouldn't be very long until he's in a home. Hopefully, he can get into the new long-term care unit in Carbonear."

"That's nonsense. She's not doing her job."

Olivia didn't respond. Nick made a mental note to call

the social worker after he left to drive home.

"I can't believe I let him talk me into this," she said, swinging her arms around her, gesturing at the house. "What was I thinking?"

"If you want to move into a small unit in town, we can help," Nick said, although by "we" he meant his sister, and by "help" he meant she'd pay for it.

His mom considered this briefly but was soon overwhelmed by emotion.

"I'm so stupid," Olivia said, fighting back tears.

Nick wasn't sure what to do. In his entire life, he'd seen his mother cry five times. Three of which were in the past year since his dad had been diagnosed with Alzheimer's. This was officially the fifth. The count still hadn't exceeded one hand.

"I should've listened to you and Alison," she continued. "I should've left him in the hospital after he fell. I don't know why I thought I could do this."

"Hindsight is 20/20," Nick offered. "You did what you thought was best for dad."

No longer able to hold it back, Olivia sobbed. Nick briefly put a hand on her shoulder. She flinched despite her best attempt to hide it. He retracted his hand and sat a bit closer. Unsure of what to say, he chose silence, hoping that his presence was enough. Alison would have known what to say. She always managed to find the right words. Or at least, his parents were always keen to accept them.

"I never should have gone teaching in Stephenville," she said.

Nick didn't know how to respond to that. Olivia snapped out of it after realizing what she'd said.

"I didn't mean that," she said.

"It's OK," Nick said. He stood up.

"Are you leaving?" Olivia said. "I'm sorry I said that."

"Don't worry about it. I got some stuff to do back in town. Call me if you need anything."

Olivia stepped towards him and reached an arm around him for a brief, stiff embrace. These awkward hugs usually only came three times a year: his birthday, her birthday, and Christmas. She must have been really upset.

"I love you," she muttered softly.

"I love you, too," he said, then turned and went out the door.

He got in his car and drove to the lookout over Harbour Grace. In the centre of the bay, the rusted *SS Kyle* sat permanently docked, trapped between the fingers of the headlands. Inland, beside an Irving, was a statue of Amelia Earhart standing next to a model plane, commemorating the flight she'd taken from there to Europe. Turning to personal history, his mind replayed a memory from when he was around eleven years old. He and his dad were hiking, portaging a canoe across an island, carrying backpacks full of camping gear. The terrain was challenging, typical Newfoundland barrens, full of bog and boulders. Nick stepped in some mud, which swallowed his leg up to his knee. He dropped and let go of the canoe, and it came down hard on the top of his head. He started crying then. Fred lay down his end of the canoe to check on Nick. The look of pity on his father's face was burned in Nick's memory. It wasn't an angry look, just one of resignation, a realization that this kid wasn't going to live up to his father's expectations. A look that told him he wasn't enough.

He took out his phone and called Fred's social worker.

"Hello, Sandra speaking," she answered.

"Hi, this is Nick O'Keefe," he said. "Fred's son."

"Hello, Nick, what can I do for you?"

"I'm calling to follow up on my dad's application for long-term care."

"Yes, it's been filed."

"I was wondering if you have a timetable on when he might be able to get in somewhere."

"Hard to say. He's on the waiting list now. Could be another two months at least."

"My mom said you told her it would be soon."

"Sometimes people hear what they want to hear."

Nick was quiet. An acidic rage filled his throat. He needed to get off the phone before he said something awful to this useless woman.

"I'm doing all I can for your father," Sandra continued. "I really am. Sorry."

Nick hung up the phone. He rolled down the window to get some cool air into the car.

When his dad had first been diagnosed with Alzheimer's, he'd expected to be given some kind of direct pathway into the bosom of the state's care. Instead, he and his family were confronted by a Kafkaesque wall of indifference. Healthcare only offered a couple hours a day of assisted living, and then they couldn't get anyone to come all the way out to Cachot Cove. That frustrated Nick the most.

All these baymen complaining about no jobs, and yet no one would come work for them. At least, that's what his mom told him. It was entirely possible she used that as an excuse not to get any help and maintain her martyrdom. It was the house, that goddamn house. The locals were afraid of it. That's why his parents had gotten it for so cheap. He had to admit, though, that some strange things had happened during the renovations. A mason fell off the scaffold working on the chimney, a roofer fell, too, and an electrician got shocked and had to be rushed to the emergency in Carbonear. And then, of course, his father's dementia had come on so fast and sudden. It was like one day he was getting dates and places mixed up and the next he was talking about going down to the pond to play ice hockey with his father who'd been dead for nearly fifty years.

Nick shivered and rolled the window back up. His rage had subsided enough to drive safely. He was too distracted to focus on his Roman history podcast, so he put NOFX back on.

* * *

Charlotte shook Nick awake.

"It happened again," she said.

Nick stirred and could see in the hallway that the light was on. He picked up his phone: 3:33 am.

"Sorry," he said, adjusting his eyes to the semi-lit room. "I think you were right about stress causing sleepwalking."

"No, you didn't get out of bed. I was cuddled into your back and would've noticed if you'd gotten up. I really think there's someone in the apartment."

He was about to dismiss this when he heard something from the kitchen. It was the sound of a chair moving. They both sat up straight in the bed.

"Stay here," he said.

"Should I call 911?"

"Not yet. Have your phone ready. I'll call out."

Nick got out of bed, put on some pyjama pants, and crept to the spare room, which he used as an office. He'd spent much of his time during unemployment in this glorified broom closet pretending to be a writer. Much to his surprise, he'd managed to produce a 90,000-word manuscript for a historical novel about Rasputin and the Russian revolution. Charlotte had expressed dutiful encouragement with each chapter he'd shown her, and after he was done, he sent it off to an agent. This was three months ago now. While he'd never admit it, he harboured secret dreams that this would blast him off into the rarefied orbit of successful authors. For now, though, he was stranded on a desert island, waiting for a ship to come along, having found his message in a bottle floating amidst a sea of other talented amateurs and their bottled manuscripts.

He sought an iron spike his dad had given him years ago after he'd discovered it jogging along the trails of the old railroad tracks. It sat near some of Nick's favourite books, titles like *Lenin's Tomb, The Gulag Archipelago*, and *The Brothers Karamazov*. He doubted whether he could club a cat with the thing, but it was the only weapon he had at the ready. Armed and poised to stab a vampire like Van Helsing, he ventured downstairs but wasn't prepared for what he saw. Fred was sitting on a bar stool at their tiny kitchen counter. He wore a set of yellow oilskins and a nor'easter like some kind of Halloween fisherman costume.

"Dad?" Nick asked. As he spoke, he was overcome with the stench of salted fish.

"Don't come after us," his dad warned. Always an assured and confident man, there was a nervous intensity in Fred's eyes Nick had never seen before, and it made him anxious.

"What are you talking about? How did you get here?"

"Your mother and I, we're gone. Let us go."

At that moment, Nick realized that it had been a year since he'd heard his dad speak.

"Everything alright?" Charlotte called out.

"Yeah, it's fine," Nick turned around and answered.

When he turned back to the kitchen, his father was gone. Nick took a deep breath, releasing the tension in his chest and neck, then went around the apartment, turning off the lights. When he got back in bed, he lay the spike on his nightstand.

"What was that all about?" Charlotte asked.

"I have no idea. Maybe I got up to use the bathroom and turned the lights on because I was half asleep or something."

"You didn't get out of bed, I'm telling you."

Nick didn't respond.

"I heard you talking to someone," she continued.

Unless he wanted to stay up for the rest of the night while she needled him, he was going to have to be straight with her.

"I saw dad in the kitchen."

"What?"

"He spoke to me. Then, after you called out," Nick snapped his fingers, "he was gone."

"What did he say?"

"He said not to go after him and mom."

"What do you think that means?"

"I have no idea."

"Maybe it was his fetch."

"What's a fetch?"

"It's a spectral double of a living person. Usually an omen of impending death."

Nick grinned. "Stop trying to make fetch happen."

Charlotte crossed her arms across her chest and stared at the ceiling, pouting.

"I'm only joking," Nick cooed. "OK, so, you're telling me dad is going to die soon?"

"I don't know. If they appear in the morning instead of night, it could mean a long life."

"It's nearly 4 am, so is that morning or night?"

Charlotte shot him a cross look.

"You know I don't believe in that stuff," Nick said.

"He could be trying to warn you."

"OK, but warn me against what? He said 'don't come after us.' What does that mean? It's not like they're lost in the Amazon."

Nick's phone rang. They looked at each other. He picked it up and saw that it was his sister.

"Hello?"

"Something's happened to mom," Alison said.

"What's going on? What's wrong?"

"I think she had a stroke. The ambulance is there taking her away to the hospital. I need you to go look after dad."

* * *

When Nick arrived at the merchant's mansion in Cachot Cove, there was a strange woman there with his dad who he'd never met before. She appeared to be around ninety years old but had the presence of someone thirty years younger.

"I called the ambulance for your mom," she explained. "I should have explained about your father, but it was all I could think to do at the time. They're going to send another ambulance to get him once they have a bed figured out for him. Either at the hospital in Carbonear or in the long-term care home."

"Are they taking my mom to Carbonear?" Nick asked.

"Yes, they did. I have to get going now. Sorry about your mother."

"Thank you so much."

The woman seemed eager to get out of the house. Nick remembered how the locals believed it was haunted, so he didn't want to hold her up. He felt a greater sense of appreciation realizing she'd done the right thing despite being afraid. That's when he heard Fred smacking his stomach.

The room stunk. It stunk like shit. Enough to turn Nick's stomach. Maybe that's why the woman was so eager to get out of there. Standing before his father, Nick was at first in denial, hoping maybe it was just a really bad fart. But the smell was undeniable. He lifted the blanket and saw watery shit leaking from his father's diaper. Fred clapped his stomach while keeping that blank expression on his face.

"You've got to be fucking kidding me," Nick said. "You had to wait until I got here, didn't you? I bet if you knew Alison was coming you would've tightened right up. Couldn't have daddy's little girl getting her hands dirty."

Fred stared through him, showing no sign any of these words were registering.

"Maybe if I'd stuck with hockey, you wouldn't have me cleaning up after you, huh?"

Nick felt the rage drain out of him as he stared at his father, helpless and confused like a baby in a crib. All that was left now was a yawning void. The ambulance would be by soon to hopefully take Fred to the nursing home, and Nick couldn't let him go there covered in his own filth. He accepted this last indignity as probably his final caregiving role as a son.

"Alright, dad," he said. "One last time."

Nick stretched some latex gloves over his hands and got to work. He pulled off his dad's diaper to reveal a brown slurry covering his crotch and thighs. There was just no getting used to seeing his dad's dick lying there like a dead trout. What was perhaps worse, though, was seeing Fred's thighs, which were once the thick, muscular legs of a hockey player and marathon runner, reduced to gaunt sprigs. Starting with the toilet paper, he went through about half a roll getting the worst of it, then used baby wipes for the remaining stains. The sheets were all going to have to be tossed, there was no helping it. Once everything was clean and tidy, he got his dad into a new diaper. Then, just as Nick pulled away, Fred grabbed his wrist. Nick looked into his father's eyes and saw the same intensity he'd seen in his dreamlike vision earlier. That old strength that could drive a nail through a board with ease was back. Nick waited for his father to speak, but Fred eventually released his son's wrist and lay back down, staring at the wall and smacking his stomach. Nick sprayed some Febreze around the house then hauled the bag of dirty sheets outside. He took a moment to appreciate the fresh air.

It was around 8 am now and he could see Cachot Cove stirring awake. Faint plumes billowed from chimney stacks into the frosty air. He wondered where that old woman lived. Nick hadn't even thought to ask for her name. Bit of an overwhelming situation so it wasn't like he was being rude. She had to live close by to have seen his mother was in trouble. In fact, now that he thought about it, she must have called the ambulance at around 3 am. How could she have known something was going on? Was she in the house? Maybe she was an overnight caregiver his mother had neglected to tell him about. But she seemed too old to be doing that kind of work.

Nick didn't have time to think about this much longer as he saw an ambulance enter through Cachot Cove's blasted rock. It soon pulled into the driveway.

"We're taking him to the LTC in Carbonear," the paramedic explained when they got out.

A fresh sense of indignity swelled in Nick's chest. After all that hemming and hawing, a bed was now suddenly available. They had to wait until after calamity struck to finally do something.

"Nice work," the other paramedic said, admiring Nick's tattoos. "Tribal?"

"Uhh...well, Celtic."

Nick was taken aback by this casual familiarity given the circumstances, but he supposed walking in and out of people's tragedies was just a part of the job for paramedics. They went about their duties as if they were loading a pile of lumber at Kent's. Nick wasn't upset; it wasn't like they were careless or unprofessional—quite the opposite. But the ho-hum workmanship felt surreal. And as they lifted his father into a stretcher then into the rig, he wrestled with whether or not he should feel ashamed by the sense of relief he felt.

CHAPTER TWO

Following Alison's lead, Nick sloshed through wet snow, tramping from his car into The Dock. Entering through the doorway, he felt like he was walking into a giant bag of salt and vinegar chips. The warm hug of the kitchen's heat filled the restaurant along with "Music and Friends" by Simani. He approached the nearest empty table, but Alison grabbed his arm.

"Hold on," she said.

"For what?" he asked.

She pointed towards her favourite booth, where Great Big Sea had once gotten their photo taken. At the moment, there was a middle-aged couple sitting there, digging through what looked to be a fresh couple plates of fish and chips.

"They probably just started eating," Nick said.

"I'm going to go talk to them," Alison replied.

Before Nick could stop her, Alison approached their table. He couldn't hear what she was saying, but he watched as the perplexed expressions on the couple's faces gradually turned sympathetic. They picked up their plates and shifted to another table.

"What did you tell them?" Nick asked.

"That this is where we used to sit with dad," she said, then eventually added: "And we're celebrating the first anniversary of his death."

"I can't believe you," Nick said. The booth's vinyl cushioning squeaked and sighed as they sat down.

"What? I wasn't completely dishonest—in a manner of speaking. Besides, it's tradition. And today of all days."

Nick could see the tiredness in Alison's eyes. And not just a physical tiredness from a lack of sleep; it was a mental, even spiritual, fatigue. He imagined he looked pretty much the same after the last couple of days driving back and forth to Carbonear, taking turns standing vigil over their mother in the hospital and their dad in the LTC. Nick wasn't sure what they were supposed to be doing during these shifts—he just sat there reading or absent-mindedly watching television—but their presence seemed necessary. It was simply what one did in these types of situations. Fortunately, today some aunts and uncles had stepped up and took over watch duty.

A woman with stringy grey hair approached their booth armed with a pencil and notepad. There was no nametag on her shirt, and she didn't offer one. She raised her eyebrows as a gesture to show she was ready to take their orders.

"Can I get a hamburger with pineapple and jalapenos?" Alison asked.

The server frowned, unimpressed. "We don't got nothing like that, honey."

"Alright, one-piece fish and chips, no dressing or gravy, with a diet ginger ale."

Nick ordered a two-piece meal with dressing and gravy and a Pepsi.

"What are you getting on with?" he asked Alison when the server left. "This isn't Toronto."

"You should try it sometime. It's really good."

The server came back to their table and laid two sheets of paper down with some cutlery and their drinks.

"How's the job search going?" Alison asked.

Nick shrugged.

"Are you following up with your applications? That's important, y'know."

"You're worse than mom. Does that even work?"

"Well, that's what everyone says."

Nick looked out the window. Dish-water clouds filtered a dull mid-day light, barely illuminating streets filled with ugly, hard snow covered with black and grey dirt. It was almost March now, so it would be like this for at least another thirty days. He always found this time of year so draining. The novelty of winter and the Christmas/New Year's high was well worn off by this point. Now he was waiting for the clocks to finally jump ahead, so he could look forward to some sunshine after 5 pm. Not like he had much else to look forward to.

"Since you have no leads, I have a proposition for you," Alison said.

"This should be interesting," Nick replied.

"You should buy the house."

"What house?"

"Mom and dad's."

"The merchant's mansion? Why?"

"You could finish fixing it up and sell it. Or run it like

a B&B like mom and dad wanted."

"Here's your food," the server announced as she laid the plates on their table.

Like their dad, Nick went heavy with lemon juice and tartar sauce on his fish. He ate his fries first before they got soggy under the dressing and gravy. He left the fish alone while he worked on the fries because the batter got crunchier if allowed to sit for a moment. Alison was doing this thing where she sprinkled salt and pepper into her hand then distributed it over her food by rubbing her palms together. Nick stared at her.

"All shakers are different," she explained. "This helps me normalize sodium intake." She took a bite of her fish and rolled her eyes back. "Ugh, so good. It's been too long."

"It's really the best on the island, like dad used to say. The batter here actually has character and texture. Newfoundlanders have such bland palates."

"So," Alison said after they were halfway through their food, "what do you think?"

"About the house?"

"Yeah."

"I think I have no idea about fixing up a house."

"That's easy to learn. There's so much stuff on TV and online. You're good at researching."

"I don't have the kind of money to take on a mortgage or pay for materials."

"I'll spot you the down payment and co-sign the loan. And I'll chip in on materials or whatever. Just pay me back when you flip it. Interest free."

"Why? What's the big deal?"

"Mom is going to need homecare, or she may even have to go into a retirement home, depending on how bad this stroke is. The money from the sale can help support her. Or best-case scenario, if she recovers, it would be nice to still have the house in case she wants to visit it. She might even still want to continue the project."

"I'm not so sure about that last part," Nick said.

"Why do you say that?" Alison asked.

"Pretty sure mom hates the house, and only did it because dad wanted to."

Alison nodded, looking as if she hadn't really considered this. A rare moment of acquiescing to Nick's judgment, however minor.

"It really was dad's baby," she agreed. "I guess it was his way of reconnecting with his roots. He couldn't let go of that outport lifestyle."

"When I was there the day before mom had her stroke, she said she wished she hadn't gone to Stephenville to teach."

"That's sad. Part of the bargaining stage of grieving."

"Can you grieve for someone who isn't dead?"

Neither had an answer to that question.

Nick scooped up the last his fish along with the dressing and gravy and heaved it all into his mouth, lingering on the savoury flavour. Alison then piled the last third of her meal onto his. He doused ketchup over everything to account for the lack of gravy.

"Don't you think it's funny that dad stopped going to church but still insisted on eating fish on Fridays?" Nick asked.

"I never did understand the no-meat-on-Friday thing,"

Alison answered. "Fish is meat."

"Technically it's no warm-blooded meat on Fridays as an act of penitence. We could eat reptile if we wanted."

"Didn't that start because a Pope was bribed by fish merchants or something? Crocodile is actually really good, by the way."

"Nah, that's a myth," Nick said. "It's funny, too, that dad was so healthy but loved fish and chips. Remember when he scraped the icing off his fiftieth birthday cake?"

Alison laughed. "I guess dad was just into the tradition. It was like a little treat he allowed himself."

"An excuse to have fish and chips. It's like he flipped the concept of penitence in a way. Like he was subverting his Catholic heritage."

Alison smirked and looked out the window. Nick knew she was jealous he'd produced that insight.

"I think it's amazing that dad lived so healthy and still got sick," she said. "If you look at those guidelines they give seniors to help avoid Alzheimer's, dad did all of it: be active, avoid smoking and drinking, eat well, have hobbies, be involved in your community. He did it all! And not even sixty-years old. Still so young."

"It happened so fast, too," Nick agreed. "It was like one day he started acting strange and then he was bedridden."

"We probably should've known something was up when he started drinking a two-litre bottle of Pepsi a day."

"Yeah, what was up with that?"

"People with dementia don't experience food like they used to, so they crave strong flavours, almost like a toddler."

Fred's monkish asceticism was no match for biology, Nick thought to himself and took a final sip from his tin of Pepsi.

"When will you be going back to Toronto?" he asked.

"Once mom is settled, and we have the house figured out." She looked at him pointedly.

"It's a big thing to take on. And I'll have to talk it over with Charlotte."

"You could write a book about it. The history of the house itself, the merchant family, and the community. Mom told me the old guy that lived there, Alistair Moore, was really into the occult. Sounds like a real character. And you could write about learning how to become a handyman and helping out your family. I can totally visualize it. It would be so good."

"Newfoundland history isn't really my thing."

"Well, what about that Russian historical novel? How's that coming along?"

"By the way," he said, quickly changing the subject. "Why did they call you first when the ambulance took mom?"

"I'm her next of kin now that dad is sick."

"But you're all the way out in Toronto. Wouldn't it make more sense for me to be her next of kin for emergencies?"

"I don't know. I guess mom feels more comfortable having me there."

Nick was silent.

"Don't be like that," she said. "You know how mom is. She doesn't want to worry her baby boy."

"That's bullshit. I'm the one who stuck around to help."

He at once regretted the words after they'd slipped from his mouth. Alison's eyes flared with indignation.

"What are you trying to say? That I walked out on you guys?"

"No—"

"That I abandoned you?"

"That's not what I meant."

"What do you want? A medal? You talk about mom being a martyr, but you're just like her."

Alison got up, pulled a fifty from her purse, and dropped it on the table. She left before Nick could say anything else. His head spun by how fast the conversation had deteriorated, but they were both feeling pretty burnt out, so he couldn't hold it against her that much. There had to be some truth to what he'd said to have gotten that reaction out of her. Alison, once an elite basketball player, knew that a good offence was a good defence, so that performative outrage was an instinctual reaction to keep that line of attack subdued. He supposed that she'd gotten so used to being the golden child that she didn't know how to handle him encroaching on her territory, especially after years of establishing himself in the role of the fuck-up. One thing that really stood out to him was when she said he was just like their mother and her martyrdom. Alison often made these sorts of pronouncements like she was trying to highlight the deeper connections he had to the family despite not being genetically related, which he appreciated in an odd way. Nick often felt this push and pull between him and his family. However alienated he may feel from them, like a cone growing on the side of their little triangle, they still insisted they were all one square.

The server chose that moment to approach the booth. "Anything else?"

Nick sat and stared at his empty plate.

"Slice of bakeapple pie and ice cream, please."

* * *

Nick could feel a pinch in his shoulder that started at the joint and travelled both up into his neck and down into his elbow. Now in his late twenties, he supposed that these little aches and pains didn't simply take care of themselves anymore. He noticed, too, that his love handles didn't take care of themselves either. For so long, he'd grown accustomed to eating whatever he wanted and sweating it all out in the gym. Now his metabolism was conspiring against him, too. He racked the bar and sat up from the bench. Two-hundred and change for ten reps was pretty good. All that fish and chips in his belly made him feel sluggish, but the salt was giving him a great pump. He looked at himself in the long mirror and admired his swollen chest and arms. The bulging beer belly was less impressive. However, he refused to buy new, larger gym clothes because the ill-fit forced him to work harder. Every time he had to pull his tank-top down over his stomach, he swore to himself he'd start eating better.

There was a group of young girls working out, likely undergrads. They paid Nick no mind. Not too long ago, he'd catch one sneaking a glance at him, but that happened rarely nowadays. Not even his tattoos were a novelty anymore. Maybe they'd be impressed if he told them he'd managed to get an op-ed published in *The Globe and Mail* about Vladimir Putin and the legacy of *Grozny* tsars. Maybe. It had been good enough to get a first date with Charlotte when she came into the Writing Centre two years ago for help on her chemistry term paper.

His phone buzzed. The home screen showed a notification from Gmail. He pulled it down and saw that it was from the agency he'd sent his manuscript. He pulled the notification down a little more to read the first chunk of the email's text: *Dear Nick, Thank you for giving us the opportunity to read your book, however we regret to inform you that…* He didn't bother to read the rest. With a thirty-pound dumbbell in each hand, he focused all his attention on bicep curls, embracing the painful swelling in his arms. Sweat dripped from his head down into his lips, and he could taste its salty flavour. It wasn't fair. None of it. Nothing went his way. The bullshit just kept piling up. He used the anger and frustration to push himself beyond failure. When his arms were too tired to lift the thirty-pound dumbbells, he picked up twenties and did more reps, then ten, until his arms were like two strands of spaghetti noodles.

After his workout was over, he got in the sauna to sweat out the rest of the salt from lunch. He felt the lactic acid drain from his chest and biceps. The endorphin rush following a hard workout beat any anti-anxiety meds on the market. As he breathed in the sauna's smoky, cedar aroma, the residual tension from his argument with Alison and the disappointment of his manuscript's rejection drained away, and he started to gain some perspective. His sister was right about pretty much everything she'd said. Not only would he be helping his family, but this could also be the professional break he'd need. The experience could be used as a memoir like *A Heartbreaking Work of Staggering Genius*. Then the profit from the sale could help to continue focusing on his writing. He just had to sell Charlotte on it all. They'd be saving a ton of money by leaving the apartment and living in Cachot Cove. Two hours wasn't that long of a commute.

He left the gym and swung by MUN's chemistry building to pick up Charlotte.

"Are you hungry?" he asked when she got in the car.

"Starving," she answered.

"What do you want to get?" he asked, hoping she'd say Mary Browns.

"We're going to my parents', remember?"

"Shit," Nick let slip before he could stop himself. All the mental exhaustion had really eroded his filter.

"Don't sound so excited."

"I just forgot, that's all."

It was a small supper to celebrate her younger sister Emily getting a scholarship from UBC. Charlotte's family had a nice place, but it was in Paradise, which Nick considered the armpit of Newfoundland. He liked Charlotte's parents. They were warm, generous, and...relaxed. That's the best word Nick could think of to describe them. Never in a rush, never browbeating their kids with neediness, never counting other people's money. It always felt like they had enough. Charlotte and Emily played sports and did well in school growing up, but there didn't seem to be the same pressure he and Alison had endured. They were able to thrive because they were comfortable in their sense of security and abundance. It was enough for them to just participate and thrive, no external pressure for all-star teams or valedictorian. For Nick and his family, there was always a deficiency, a manic need to achieve, achieve, achieve. For what? To what end? They were both middle-class families. It wasn't about money or status. So why did one feel so different from the other? This was the source of Nick's resentment, that he'd inherited this bottomless, insatiable lack. There was something wrong with him, and his parents had tried to stuff this hole with achievements. But unlike Alison, who seemed to thrive under this heavy-handedness, he resisted, so Fred and Olivia just pushed harder. And the harder they pushed, the harder he resisted.

Her family also had a tradition of talking a lot during supper, something he wasn't fond of either. It was a struggle not to just zone out in the middle of the conversations. At least her mom was a great cook. The first course was roasted tomato soup. He was relishing the peppery, basil flavour when he realized Charlotte's mom was talking to him.

"I'm sorry?" he said.

"I was asking how your parents are doing?" she replied.

"They're alright," he answered. She smiled at him, waiting for him to elaborate. When he didn't, Charlotte's father awkwardly changed the subject, focusing his attention on Emily's boyfriend.

Nick was grateful to have escaped the limelight. How was he supposed to answer a question like that? *How are your parents doing?* Every mutual acquaintance of his family he ran into asked that question. How the fuck do you think they're doing? They're both goddamn vegetables for Christ's sake. And he hated that scrunched up sympathetic look they made. *If you really wanna know, go visit them.* That's what he wanted to tell them. *See for yourself.* It's not that he thought these people were insincere, he was sure they genuinely cared, but didn't they realize it's not exactly an endearing topic to discuss with every Tom, Dick, and Harry that once taught, volunteered, or had some kind of passing relationship with his parents? He felt like posting and pinning an FAQ to his Facebook page like a press release for all these busybodies.

Worse, he could sometimes see some people had a ghoulish fascination with his parents' fate, especially among those near their age. Perhaps his parents were like a *memento mori* for them, a harbinger of their own fates. The rise of dementia among boomers was unprecedented. He couldn't blame them for being both anxious and curious about what could be awaiting them. Robin Williams had the right idea as far as Nick was concerned. If a doctor ever gave him the dementia diagnosis, he was going to go straight home, pour himself a scalding hot bath, get those veins nice and juicy, then open 'em right up, like that scene in *The Godfather*. No one deserved the fate his father had been dealt.

He felt a hand gently squeeze his thigh. It was Charlotte. She gave him a look as if to say, "Everything alright?" He must have been scowling, deep in his own thoughts. Nick smiled back at her then did his best to feign interest in the current barnyard conversation.

Charlotte didn't say much on the drive home. Nick

could see she wasn't happy with how he'd acted during supper, but he could also see she was cutting him some slack given everything that was going on. He wondered how long he could get away with that. When they got home, Nick plopped on the couch and turned on *The Office*. They sat together, scrolling through their phones, occasionally paying attention to what was on the television.

Charlotte had her free hand resting on Nick's thigh. He wished she'd playfully slide it up towards his crotch, like how it used to be when they'd first started dating. They were at the point in their relationship now when they didn't have to be so flirty when initiating sex, which should be a feature not a bug, but he couldn't help missing that early excitement. It would ruin the fantasy to just take her hand and put it where he wanted. Sometimes during sex, he'd snap out of whatever reverie he was enjoying and be confronted with the frankly unappetizing reality of what was actually happening. It seemed so ridiculous to be huffing and puffing, repeating the same movements over and over, just jamming two bodily organs together. Was this normal? Did other people think like this? Maybe that would explain all the extensive roleplaying some people do. Nurse costumes, nuns, what have you. One time Charlotte suggested getting a maid outfit, but Nick didn't understand the appeal. Obviously, there's the symbolism of subservience, but who had maids anymore these days? He wasn't some nineteenth century British Lord. Who is sustaining this outdated fantasy? It would make more sense to wear a sexy Walmart uniform. But whenever she asked him about his fetishes or anything he'd like to try, he could never really answer.

"You're awfully quiet," Charlotte remarked. "Everything OK?"

"I think I'm going to buy the merchant's mansion."

"Oh."

"Mom is going to need a lot of support and the money from the sale would have her set. And I could keep the profit after I flip it. I'd also like to write a book about the experience. Part memoir, part history of the area and the mansion."

"Was that your sister's idea?"

Nick ignored that question. "Well, what do you think?"

She took a long sip of water from the glass she was holding and suddenly looked like she was about to throw up everything she'd just eaten at her parents'.

"You're not going to like what I have to say," she said finally.

Nick waited.

"That house has bad energy."

Again, Nick waited for her to elaborate.

"I know you don't believe in this stuff, but bad things happened there, and I honestly think it's dangerous."

Nick realized that he'd anticipated this sort of answer. His sister did mention something about the previous owner being into black magic. Did Charlotte know that? She'd only been there once. Maybe there was something to all this new age nonsense after all.

"Well," he offered. "Why don't you do a cleanse or whatever?"

"I doubt that would be enough, and I'm not powerful enough to give that house what it needs."

"I really need to do this for my family. And for me. I could really use your help."

"I'm going to say something else that might upset you," she said. "I know this is a bad time to bring this up, but I have to say it."

"Go ahead."

"I don't think your family respects you. They don't respect your goals or what you're trying to achieve." She drank some more water before continuing, considering her words. "It's like they're trying to run a computer program and anything that deviates from that program must be deleted."

Nick felt like he could cry. It was such a relief to hear an outside observer articulate so clearly what he was feeling but couldn't put into words. But she didn't have all the details.

"My parents definitely put a lot of expectations on me and Alison, and they were pretty strict growing up, but I put them all through hell when I was younger, doing drugs and not making much of myself."

"Yeah, but it's not like you were some criminal. A lot of people make mistakes, but you did make something of yourself. It's not fair for them to keep punishing you like that."

It was time to put all his cards on the table if he was going to salvage this.

"There's always been a weird dynamic between me and my family because I'm adopted," he explained.

"What?" Charlotte exclaimed. "You never told me this."

"They adopted me when I was maybe five or six. I actually don't have any memories from when I was young. The earliest thing I can remember is picking a box of fries out of the garbage can at the cafeteria when I was in kindergarten. A little girl dropped it in, and I was so hungry. I could see it hadn't touched anything, so when I thought no one was looking I fished it out. A teacher caught me. She was really mad, but when I told her how hungry I was, something changed in her face. After that I think I spent some time in a group home, but the next earliest memory I can remember is like grade three, and dad got me hockey equipment for my birthday. Even then I was calling them my mom and dad."

"What about your biological parents?"

"I honestly can't remember them at all. When I turned nineteen, I got some information from the government that said I was taken from my parents because they were neglecting me. I'd been deemed a failure to thrive or something like that. The records had my parents' names, and there was an option to give them my contact information if they wanted to meet me. I said yes, but nothing came of it."

"You never met them?"

"No. For all I know they could be dead. I know it's weird to say, but I'm actually totally ambivalent about it. They obviously didn't care about me. So, as hard as my parents may seem, they definitely love me, unlike those people who made me."

This was all truth blended with lies. He'd gotten the name of his biological mother and contact information from the government, but he didn't follow up on it. And no matter how many times he insisted that he was ambivalent about it, he couldn't help dwelling on who these people were, pushing his mind to remember some details about them, imagining the different ways his life could have played out had he been raised by different people. But was a lie you told yourself then repeated to others still a lie?

"Alright," she said after some consideration. "I'll help however I can, but we're not going to move in there, are we?"

Nick had indeed planned on moving in full-time, but this was probably the best he could hope for.

"No," he said. "We'll keep the apartment."

CHAPTER THREE

Nick sat in the office while the banker—what was her job title exactly? he looked at the triangular block on her desk and saw "Tina Bryant" and underneath it read "Financial Services Representative"—talked about interest rates, renewals, a fifteen-year plan vs twenty, and how the bank calculated property taxes into his bi-weekly payments as a free service.

"I think that's the best way to go?" Alison asked Nick in an assertive tone that was phrased like a question only as a vaguely polite gesture.

"Yes, I agree," Nick concurred, not entirely sure what he was agreeing to.

Tina handed them some documents to sign with helpful little stickers pointing to where they needed to sign. Nick noticed her long, frosty pink nails, which narrowed into whitish points. Each of her wrists were cuffed with chunky bracelets accented with tiny dangling charms. She jingled every time she moved, and she talked with her hands, so it was a lot. Nick wondered how she managed to type with all that racket going on. Maybe it was meant to cast a hypnotic spell while she duped distracted mopes into signing their life away to the bank. Well, it had certainly worked this time around. Nick handed the documents back to her with his signatures all over them. He left the office, hearing her charms jangling as she filed them away.

Nick followed Alison out of the bank, his head swimming with numbers. The brisk winter air felt refreshing.

"When this is all over and you sell the house," Alison said, "you guys should come to Toronto. I have a spare room in my condo you could stay in while you find a spot. There's plenty of jobs at magazines for you. Or maybe an internship to get you started."

"We'll see," Nick said. "Charlotte has a good job at the lab."

"Then you can at least experience spring," Alison continued, not registering what Nick had said.

"People who move to the mainland always say that."

"It's so true though. You have no idea how rejuvenating it is to see and smell the blooming flowers after all that snow. Winter in Newfoundland is hard enough. To have to go through the prolonged agony of April here is just torture. I can't do it anymore. Come to Toronto and see for yourself. Trust me, you'll feel reborn."

Alison was often extolling the virtues of the Big Smoke to Nick. He figured she was trying to convince herself that she'd made the right choice moving there. The fact that she'd invited him to come stay with her in her condo was puzzling since she kept her personal life locked away in an impenetrable vault. Nick figured all Alison did was work, yoga, and long walks on the weekends. Maybe now that he was no longer needed to keep an eye on their parents, she didn't want to keep feeling like he was there holding down the fort while she was selfishly chasing her career as an investment banker on Bay Street.

They got into his car and took the highway out of St. John's towards Carbonear. It wasn't snowing, but the strong winds blew powder onto the roads and peppered the windshield with flakes. It was after 10 am now so the rush of people coming into town and people leaving town for Long Harbour was over.

"What's mom going to do now that she doesn't have dad to take care of anymore?" he asked.

"Start living her life, I hope," Alison replied. "Mom is such an intelligent and capable woman, but she's used her family as an excuse not to ask more out of life."

"I know what you mean. It's like she micromanaged our lives to distract herself from anything else."

"After her miscarriage I guess she got pretty obsessed with her kids."

"I didn't know mom had a miscarriage."

"Yeah, a couple years after I was born, they tried to have another kid. It was pretty bad. She had to have a hysterectomy. Why do you think they adopted you?"

"I knew mom couldn't have kids after you, but I didn't know that was why."

Nick reflected on this as the still-frozen boggy landscape of the TCH rolled by. It was strange to consider his parents as individuals separate from his own life, that they were people with their own baggage. It didn't help that they'd always presented themselves as insufferable know-it-alls who never made mistakes. But that wasn't entirely their fault; they'd been high school teachers their whole lives. It came with the trade. Now he was peeking behind the curtain to discover the Great and Terrible Wizard of Oz was really just two mere mortals pushing and pulling levers. Well, they weren't operating the machine anymore. Both of them were floating away in the hot air balloons of their broken brains, and Nick was still trapped in Oz with no magic ruby slippers.

"It makes me sad that I never asked dad how he felt about it all," Alison said, staring out the car's window.

"I don't think he would've been able to articulate much of a response."

"At first he could have, when he was initially diagnosed. There was a period there for a while where he was still pretty lucid. I never thought to say to him, 'How do you feel about this? Are you afraid? Are you angry? Sad?' I was too scared, I guess. He was being strong for us when we should have been strong for him."

"I'm sure he just would've said something like, 'What odds, by. Nothing to be done.' That's what he said whenever things went bad."

"He had such grace dealing with things out of his control. Something we could learn from."

Yes, it was all well and good to talk about handling yourself with grace when you were 3,000 kilometres away. Their mother had always sought Alison's calm, objective counsel over the phone during the more dramatic moments of their father's illness. Alison deciphered all the doctors' jargon and navigated the terrible terrain of acquiring care, always able to smooth things out. But she was never there in the flesh, to change diapers, to see their mother collapse in a fit of nerves, or watch their father slap his stomach for hours, trying to communicate a thought that was now shrouded behind the plaques and tangles inside his brain. Yes, grace was something one could talk about while earning over $300,000 in a posh office looking over Lake Ontario, not when you were laid off because Newfoundland has bottomed out on yet another natural resource, leaving the job market a barren wasteland while you wait for your employment insurance to run out.

The Veterans Memorial Highway dipped into Carbonear. The town spread out to the right side of the main thoroughfare towards the bay. Carbonear Island, its eighteenth century wooden fortifications long since decayed, stood watch over the Atlantic, ready should any French fleets attempt more raids. Nick turned off the main road and made his way towards the general hospital, where their mother was staying, and the long-term care facility, where their dad was. Indicative of the province's present health priorities, the LTC unit was roughly double the size of the hospital.

"I'll go see mom first, if you want to see dad," Alison suggested.

"Sure," Nick replied.

He drove up to the hospital's entrance.

"By the way," Alison said. "Uncle Jim is in with dad."

She promptly shut the door and rushed into the hospital to get out of the wind.

"Well played, sis," Nick muttered to himself.

He flicked over to the LTC home and got a parking space. The walk from his car to the facility was short but long enough for the cold wind off the bay to smack his cheeks pink. The new facility, Nick had to admit, was pretty swanky. The sort of infrastructure Newfoundland-ers weren't used to seeing in the province. There was new furniture, plenty of glass windows, and no paint peeling off the walls. Nick thought of the many make-shift aque-ducts made of tarps, plastic, and duct tape at Memorial University, draining filthy water from pipes down Byzan-tine paths into dirty buckets. This, however, was a clean, well-lighted place. It gave him a modicum of comfort that his father was at least somewhere nice.

Nick made his way to his father's room, which he shared with another man. Mr. Anthony, his name was— at least Nick was pretty sure that's what it was. In the two weeks since his dad first got here, he had yet to see any visitors for his roommate. Uncle Jim was beside Fred. They were both silently watching hockey highlights. Uncle Jim flashed Nick a brief smile and nodded gravely.

"Hi, Uncle Jim," Nick offered. "How are you?"

"Oh, y'know," Uncle Jim managed, "tough circum-stances."

Nick pulled up a chair and the three of them watched three pundits talk about what teams had a chance to battle for the last couple playoff spots. Montreal's season had been over after Price got injured. At least they'd qualify for a decent draft pick. No one could compete for Toronto's race to the bottom, though. They were tanking hard for that first overall pick.

"Play at all these days?" Uncle Jim asked.

"Nah," Nick replied. "Not since high school."

He'd probably seen his Uncle Jim a dozen times since high school, and each time he'd ask if he still played. Be-

fore that, it had felt like Uncle Jim was a regular part of
his life, but now he realized that's because his uncle was
at just about every one of his games. Aside from that, he
wasn't around much. Hockey was the only thing Uncle
Jim seemed comfortable talking about. Nick understood
that when Uncle Jim wasn't delivering the mail, he was
at his local dive watching either the Canadiens or the
Blue Jays, or whatever else was on the television. Jim was
Fred's only sibling still living in Newfoundland. Their
three sisters were scattered between Ontario and Alberta.
The only one Nick really kept track of was his Aunt Becky,
who lived in Fort Mac and regularly made unhinged Facebook posts about the oil industry, vaccines, and whatever
conspiracy theory was popular at the time. It cracked him
up. With the American election approaching, she was really juiced up about Trump and the Mexican border wall.
Nick wondered how many Mexicans made it up to Fort
Mac.

"Your dad always thought you could have made it to
the major juniors," Uncle Jim said. "Always said you had
the best vision on the ice. Never panicked with the puck,
especially in your own end. Just needed to work on your
skating."

Nick was surprised by this. Not the latter part—his
dad criticized his skating all the time—but he'd never
heard that initial line of praise before. Nick had always
secretly prided himself on his strong first pass. Never allowing himself to ring the puck around the boards or toss
it into the neutral zone, he always managed to get it to a
forward moving up the ice or over to his fellow defence-
man. He never realized how much insight his dad had

into his game. Fred usually just told him that if he were a better skater, he could carry it out himself.

He felt a combination of guilt and resentment, a familiar cocktail when thinking about his family. Guilt because here was a bond between him and his dad he'd never realized until now when it was too late. Guilt for all the nasty arguments they'd had when Nick insisted he wasn't going to play anymore, was quitting AAA, the high school team, everything. Resentment because Fred never thought to mix some of that honey with the medicine. Resentment because his parents' default position was disapproval. Whenever he complained they were too critical, they'd respond, "Well, what do you want us to say? 'Yes, that's fine, everything's fine.' The world's not like that." True, the world could be tough, but it could be kind sometimes. You didn't have to be a hard ass 24/7. Besides, if the world is an angry and mean place, shouldn't your family be a safe haven from all that every once in a while? Pretty hard when you got to take your lumps outside and inside your house. He wished he'd had the vocabulary at the time to express that, but he was just a teenager. In real life, teens don't articulate themselves like characters on *Dawson's Creek*. They're self-absorbed, sullen, and hormonal. He wished he could've told them that he'd felt like he was stuck on a treadmill with their love dangling in front of him like a carrot on a stick, that no matter how fast or far he ran, he could never catch it. That it was never enough; he was never enough.

He looked down to his father. Fred lay in bed, turning his head back and forth between Nick and Jim like they were playing ping pong. There seemed to be a sense of recognition in his eyes, a recognition of recognition. That he was supposed to know who these people were but couldn't remember how or why. Nick had to turn away because it was making him dizzy. He went back to watching the television.

"I think they're going to trade Subban in the offseason," Uncle Jim said.

"Oh yeah?" Nick answered.

Uncle Jim nodded gravely. "Just you watch."

Nick was actually a little relieved that his father had given up the last semblances of conversation. It was painful to have to answer the same questions over and over again. "What's the weather like? Are the waves choppy?" He'd become trapped in some memory loop of when he was young and the few summers he'd spent in the cod fishery before moving to Stephenville. The worst was when he laughed or smiled, and Nick could see the little black ridges his teeth had been reduced to thanks to all the sugar he'd punished them with over the span of just a year.

"What they should do," Uncle Jim continued, "is trade Galchenyuk now while his stock is high. That kid is a bust. Get a legit centre for next season. Price will be healthy again and we can make a real run."

Fred started smacking his stomach. Nick thought he detected a sense of panic in his father's eyes.

"What's wrong, dad?" he asked.

"He does that every now and then," Uncle Jim observed. "Any idea what it means?"

Nick shrugged. He put his hand on his dad's arm. Fred looked at him for awhile then relaxed and turned his attention back to the television. Nick's phone buzzed. He hauled it out of his coat pocket, grateful for any sort of distraction. It was Alison.

"Get over here," she said. "Mom's awake."

Nick rushed over to the general hospital to see his mom. Olivia was lying in bed and looked very weak. She squinted at Nick and didn't seem to recognize him. Alison was there with their Aunt Azalea, who, as always, looked just a touch overdressed for her setting, like she was either coming from or going to somewhere classier than she was presently. She offered him a curt smile. Nick had to admire how she'd mastered the "I have money, but I don't need to spend it on big brand names to impress you" chic indicative of upper middle-class boomers.

"I think her vision was affected by the stroke," Alison explained.

Aunt Azalea and Alison were sitting beside Olivia, so Nick bent over and took her hand. She pulled it away and looked at him, confused.

"Mom," he said, "it's Nick."

She groaned and tried to speak but no sensible words came out. That's when the doctor and nurses arrived, and everyone had to leave so they could do some tests.

"What do you think this means?" Aunt Azalea asked, directing all her attention towards Alison.

Nick stood there like a third wheel and started to miss Uncle Jim's company. The doctor emerged then and explained that she was still very weak after recovering from the stroke and was lucky to even be alive. It was too early at that point to determine any sort of timeline or how much she would eventually recover. Nick and Alison decided to swap. Aunt Azalea left.

"Your mother is so lucky to have you," Nick heard Aunt Azalea say to Alison as they walked down the hall. He was certain that "you" was exclusive to Alison.

He sat in the room with his mom and watched television. A couple gardeners on HGTV were discussing the many virtues of mulch.

"They should've had dad on to tell them all about peat," Nick said. He thought he detected a sense of recognition in her eyes, so he figured he'd keep talking. "I was over with dad at the long-term care facility. It's actually really nice over there. He's well taken care for, so you don't have to worry. Uncle Jim was there to visit. Can't even remember the last time I'd seen him. He still only wants to talk about hockey."

Olivia leaned her head forward and pressed her lips together like she was trying to speak. Nick pulled his chair closer to hear.

"Puh...puh...puh..." she tried. "Pree...preeze... preeze...st."

"Priest?" Nick said.

Olivia nodded.

"You want a priest?"

She shook her head, no.

"Mo...mo...mole...st."

"Molest?"

She nodded.

"A priest molested someone?"

Nick wondered if this was something she'd seen or heard on the news, or if this was something from her past she'd buried, which the stroke had dislodged and now floated to the surface. It felt a little wrong, like he was a black ops CIA agent in Gitmo procuring a confession under duress. But he couldn't deny he also felt a little excited, too.

"Juh…Juh…him."

"Jim? Uncle Jim? A priest molested Uncle Jim?"

She nodded then fell back to her pillow, exhausted by the effort. Nick leaned back in his chair and tried to digest this revelation. Was it even true? It would explain a lot. Pretty much everything, really. Uncle Jim seemed like such a melancholy soul, a life-long bachelor and loner. It also explained his dad's complicated relationship with the Catholic Church. He wasn't sure how to feel about this. Clearly, his mother wasn't in a proper state of mine, but he still felt like she'd needed to unburden herself of this secret and trusted him.

It was 4 pm now and starting to get dark. Alison and Nick needed to leave while they still had light on the highway.

"How was mom?" Alison asked as they made their way out of Carbonear, back towards St. John's.

"Not bad," Nick said. "She actually spoke a little. Well, she could barely get the words out, but I think I understood what she was trying to say."

"Really? What was it?"

"You're not going to believe this, but apparently Uncle Jim was molested by a priest. I'm not sure whether or not it's true because mom's state of mind is obviously not great, but it would explain a lot."

"Yeah, it's true."

"You knew?"

"Mom told me a couple years ago."

Nick gripped the steering wheel with both hands. It was a weird thing to feel possessive over, but he felt like he'd finally managed to carve out his own intimate bond with their mother, only to realize he'd actually been out of the loop to begin with. If she hadn't had her stroke, he probably would have never learned about Uncle Jim. Yet she'd trusted Alison with this information.

"Something wrong?" Alison asked.

"Mom and dad always keep me in the dark but tell you everything."

Alison shrugged. "I'm just nosier than you."

Nick couldn't disagree about that. If Alison felt like you were keeping something from her, she'd pry it out of you like a dog digging up a bone. It's part of what made her a successful investment banker, he imagined—always digging for the rationale behind the numbers. But this was only half the story. To Nick, this was more proof that his parents had a special bond with his sister that he didn't share.

"I thought that eventually I'd have an adult relationship with them," Nick said. "That they'd level with me and talk to me like an equal."

"You're too standoffish," she explained. "You have to meet them halfway."

"Their halfway mark is more like the ten-yard line."

"Sure, but you just built up this wall and stopped letting them in. You never explained why you quit hockey or waited to go to college. No one ever knew what was going on in your head."

"Because if I'd let them in, they'd only try and take

control again."

"They just wanted the best for you."

"You're telling me there's no part of your life you didn't keep from mom and dad?"

Alison kept her attention on the TCH.

"I was talking to Lanes," she said eventually. "We're on the waiting list. By the time mom is ready to leave the hospital it should be ready for her. I'm flying back to Toronto tomorrow. I can't miss any more work."

"You're leaving already?" Nick asked.

"I told you, I can't miss any more work. Besides, everything is taken care of. All you need to do is work on the house and visit mom and dad whenever you can."

They drove the rest of the way in silence. When Nick dropped Alison off at her hotel, he gripped the steering wheel tight, knowing that he was pretty much on his own from here on out.

* * *

Fred O'Keefe was lost in time. He stared at the television screen and watched himself skate around Black Duck Pond. Seven rocks, which everyone called the Seven Sisters, poked up through the ice, which he manoeuvred around as a drill. Each time he circled around, he tried to do it with more speed. The sun was setting, and it was getting difficult to see the puck as he stick-handled around the sisters. His frosty breath hung in the air as he panted. He could hardly feel his hands and feet. His clothes were damp with sweat, which sent a chill through his body when he'd start skating against the wind.

"It's getting cold," Jim complained.

"Just a few more times," Fred insisted. "Try and beat my time."

"You know I can't."

"Sure you can. You're better at stick handling than me, you just gotta skate harder. Trust yourself."

Jim did a quick circle to gather momentum then scooped up the puck and went for it. He sped through the first six sisters with ease. Fred envied his brother's effortless velocity. But then Jim slowed, afraid of catching his skate on the last Sister, the trickiest. Everyone called her the Bitch. Jim skated back around with a bashful look on his face, knowing exactly what Fred was going to say. Even though he wouldn't admit it, Fred knew Jim was the better hockey player. He just didn't have that fire in him. Or at least, not anymore. Something had diminished it. Ever since Jim started being an altar boy at church, he'd changed, become withdrawn. Maybe Father Kenney told him hockey was a sin. Whatever it was, Fred had taken it upon himself to fix whatever was broken there.

Before Fred could admonish his little brother for taking his foot off the gas at the last moment, a voice called out to them.

"Hey, boys!"

It was their father. They looked to each other with expressions of guilt. How late was it? Had they lost track of time? Jim glared at Fred with blame in his eyes.

"We were just about to come home," Jim started. "Honest!"

Patrick O'Keefe held up his hand as he shimmied across the ice. "That's fine," he said. "You go on home, Jim. I want to have a word with Fred."

Jim exchanged a puzzled look with his brother before scooting off, obedient as always. Patrick hesitated, waiting for Jim to get out of earshot. Fred started to feel anxious for whatever bad news his father seemed to be struggling to say.

"We're leaving," he said. "I got a job in Stephenville at the prison. I'm leaving in a week. You, your brother, and sisters will stay here with your mom until the start of the summer when your school is finished."

Fred stared at the ice under his skates, trying to comprehend what he'd just heard.

"I don't want to go to Stephenville," he said. It was all he could figure to say.

Patrick nodded like he knew this was exactly what Fred was going to say.

"I know it's going to be tough going to a new town and new school. But they got a great rink down there. It'll be a great opportunity for you and your brother to skate with better players."

Fred had to admit that sounded good.

"But what about the boat?" he asked. "What about the fish?"

"I'm selling the boat."

Fred was speechless.

"I'm giving up the fish," Patrick explained. "There's no future in it. I don't want you and Jim going at it either."

This was too much. Fred shook his head. "No," he said. "No, no, no. You promised I could work on the boat this summer."

"I know. I'm sorry. But you have to trust me that this

is the right decision. When you're a man with a family, you'll understand. You and your brother and sisters are smart. You can go to school and get an education. Things me and my family growing up never dreamed about. You could be a math teacher. You're good with sums." After some delay he added: "One day, you'll thank me."

"I don't want any of that. I want to be a fisherman like you and grandad."

"You're just going to have to trust me. I'm your father."

"I don't care! I'm fourteen. I can drop out of school and work if I want."

"I won't allow it."

"Fuck you!"

Patrick drew in a breath like he'd been stabbed. Fred had never cursed at his father before. They stared at each other. Hot tears dripped from Fred's eyes, briefly warming his cheeks until the frigid air stung them cold. He didn't wipe them away, refusing to acknowledge their presence. Patrick took a step towards Fred, who stood his ground. He looked down at his son's snivelling face and turned away, walking towards the bank and off the ice.

Fred circled around and drove his emotions into his skates. He dug his blades into the ice and sped across the pond like his idol, Bobby Orr. The Seven Sisters rushed towards him as he skated into the gauntlet at top speed. He kept his head up, watching where he was going, gliding around the rocks like how Bobby caught guys flat-footed, blazing past them like statues. Just as he was about to clear the last Sister, the puck rolled. He looked down briefly to settle it when his left skate clipped the Bitch. His leg shot backwards, and he nose-dived. He slid across the ice then lay still, too dazed to stand up. The metallic flavour of blood filled his mouth. He tried to push himself up, but the blood had already frozen to the ice. Panting, he managed to thaw it just enough with his warm breath to peel his face off like a strip of Velcro. He got up to a knee then took off his gloves to feel around his mouth. Despite the raw throbbing on his face, no teeth were missing, and his nose felt like it was where it should be. Blood had poured down his face and onto his sweater, so he was going to catch hell for that from his mom—on top of being saucy to his father.

His ankles ached as he pulled off his skates, and the tight muscles in his shins complained the whole walk home.

"Jesus, Mary, and Joseph!" his mom shouted as he entered the house.

Fred explained what had happened.

"Give it to me here I runs it under the tap before it stains. Little good it'll do I imagine. Your father is in the living room. Wants to have a word with you."

Watching the television, Fred knew what happened next. He didn't want to watch, but he didn't know how to change the channel. Beside him two strangers were talking in some language he didn't understand. Their faces seemed familiar, but he couldn't figure out how he knew them. He turned his attention back to the television where he watched a younger version of himself in his old house in Black Duck Cove enter the living room. His dad was sat in the rocking chair listening to the radio. But something was wrong. His glass was overturned. Fred looked down and saw melting ice cubes floating in a mix of rum and Coke. He looked up and saw his father's face frozen in a painful contortion. A scream was trapped inside him; it wouldn't come out. It was trapped in his belly. He slapped at his stomach like he had a bad case of gas, trying to force it out. But it wouldn't come.

That's when he woke up. He shot up straight in bed with a loud gasp, loud enough to wake his wife.

"What is it?" Olivia asked. "Bad dream?"

He nodded. His brow was wet with sweat. Dawn's early light was breaking in the sky. Time to wake up anyhow, Fred thought to himself. He went down to the kitchen and quickly gobbled two slices of Olivia's bread with some molasses then was out the door towards the harbour.

The sun rose over yet another beautiful day in Cachot Cove. The men were loading their gear into their boats and starting their make and break engines to *putputput* after the cod. He was doing it, living his dream. His father had been wrong. There was still a living to be had at the sea.

"Sleeping in this morning, Fred?" a man asked.

He brought some nets from Fred's shed and dropped them in the boat. But Fred didn't recognize this man. Looking around, he didn't recognize where he was either. It looked like Cachot Cove, but it didn't make any sense. He'd come there as an older man, to redo an old merchant's mansion for a bed and breakfast with his wife as a retirement project. These sorts of stages didn't exist anymore, mostly replaced by concrete government wharves and fish plants. He looked to where the merchant's mansion was supposed to be, but instead saw a great brick castle. Panic overwhelmed him. He was caught in some strange dream. The urge to scream once again overwhelmed him, but it was caught inside his stomach.

He woke up again. This time in the hospital bed. He was watching TV. A couple talking heads were discussing hockey. To the left and right of him were familiar voices. He looked around and saw his brother Jim and Nick, his son. The house, he had to warn him about the house. But the words wouldn't come, trapped inside him, deep in some prison in his stomach. He slapped and slapped but couldn't release them.

"What's up, dad?" Nick asked. Fred saw the bewildered sympathy in his son's eyes. If only there was a way to make him understand.

But the day was getting on now and he had to get to his catch. Moore would be upset if he didn't settle his account.

CHAPTER FOUR

Nick pulled into the merchant's mansion's driveway, which now belonged to him, something that made him both oddly proud and anxious. After the sale was official, he got his mom's keyset and noticed hers had an additional skeleton key that he'd never seen. Neither of his parents had shown it to him before and he wasn't sure what it opened. Holding it in his hand, he had to admit it was pretty cool, like a real old school dungeon key. The bit at the bottom looked like a little rectangular hourglass and at the top were three ornate circles, like a clover. Nick assumed it was the key for the old front door his parents had replaced.

As he surveyed the merchant's mansion, he started to appreciate his mother's frustration. What the hell had his dad been thinking? To invest practically all their retirement savings into this place was crazy. Outside a few minor home improvements, which Fred usually botched, Nick couldn't remember his dad ever expressing much of a passion for carpentry—or running a bed and breakfast for that matter. But a couple years ago when Fred and Olivia came across this place during one of their Sunday drives, Fred's imagination went wild, and he had to have it.

Eastern Health had taken away his dad's hospital bed, so the main parlour was now empty. For perhaps the first time, Nick had a chance to admire the fireplace. There was a floral design sculpted into the centre of the marble mantel flanked by two dragonflies. Aside from a few nicks, it was in excellent condition. Beneath the fireplace were hexagonal tiles, which reminded Nick of a honeycomb. Marred by some scuffing here and there, he would love to improve them and make them pop. Would that mean painting them? He made a mental note to research that. The second parlour was separated from the main by a pair of pocket doors. Nick slid them open, feeling like some aristocrat in a Dickens novel. There was only a slight bit of noise as they retreated into the walls—not bad for, what, 150 years old? This was where his mom had set up her bed. He could remember helping her haul that down from the third story attic where they'd initially set up their bedroom. At the end of the second parlour were the main bay windows. The shutters were built into the windows' frame, which Nick had never seen before. He opened them up and revealed a spectacular view of Cachot Cove harbour. It was a dreary March day with plenty of rain, drizzle, and fog, but he could imagine how it would look on a clear summer morning. He imagined himself looking out over the bay with a cup of coffee in his hand. What a place to set up a desk for writing, taking advantage of all that natural light. And when it was dark there was the chandelier above him, hanging from a wooden medallion carved into leafy flourishes. Nick could see some tiny flakes of gold that once gilded the flowers. It even had some of the original crystals still dangling from its wrought iron curlicues.

Looking out the bay window, he remembered the old woman who'd called the ambulance for his mom. She'd said she saw that Olivia was in distress. If the shutters had been closed, how did she see? Even if they were open, it was in the middle of the night. The houses of Cachot Cove were packed pretty densely, but the merchant's mansion was a good fifty meters from the nearest property. She'd have to have some pretty damn good eyes for someone who appeared to be well beyond sixty years old. Something wasn't adding up. He was planning on talking to the locals about the mansion as part of his potential book, which could give him the front he needed to do his best Lieutenant Columbo and get to the bottom of that old woman's story.

To the right of the two parlours was the dining area. Rich cherry wood wainscotting wrapped around the room. A long, ornate cast iron radiator sat by the wall, covered with the twisting patterns of vines. Another chandelier hung above where Nick imagined the table would be. This one had a medallion of grapes and fruits—in case anyone forgot this was the dining room.

Between the dining room and kitchen was an old pantry that his dad had begun converting into a small bathroom. The floor was all tore up and needed to be tiled, but at least it had a functional toilet. Maybe this would be a good place to start. He took out his phone and Googled how to tile a bathroom. The first thing he learned was that it was best to tile before fitting the toilet, so you didn't have to awkwardly cut tiles around it.

"Oh, for fuck sakes," he muttered to himself with an exasperated sigh.

This was exactly what he'd been dreading. Fred had a unique gift for doing things arse backwards. He wasn't the type to analyze a problem and consider the best course of action. Instead, he just launched himself head first. Hence why their old house had backwards kitchen taps, redundant light switches, and a panel box that looked like Dennis Hopper from *Speed* had designed it. Nick's main concern was that he'd start working on something only to realize he needed to have done something prior to that and thus needed to do it all over again. It was overwhelming. He was baffled that there were people who enjoyed this kind of work; it seemed very tedious to him. Then again, these same people probably thought it was tedious to sit around reading about Russian history.

He thought about his father and how he loved to challenge himself. As an adult, Nick could see now that it was really a skill to be able to turn any chore into a game. In the winter, when the driveway had to be cleared, Fred would try to throw each shovelful of snow over the telephone wire. (He eventually tore his rotator cuff doing this and had to buy a snowblower, for which Nick was grateful.) It was probably what made him a great athlete, particularly a runner. Fred had run the Boston, New York, London and even the original Athens marathons, consistently completing them in less than three hours. When Nick asked Fred about enduring the boredom of these long treks, his dad was confused by the question. How could something like that be boring? Every mile was an opportunity to run better than the one previous, each stretch a new challenge to overcome. Maybe that's what the merchant's mansion was to Fred: the last great challenge of his life.

At the back of the kitchen was the basement door, hidden behind some containers. Or maybe it was technically a cellar door? Very Edgar Allan Poe. People used to have cellars, now they had basements. When did that switch happen? Was there a difference? Nick imagined great big doors outside a house set at an angle. The kind in horror movies. Those were cellar doors, which was disappointing because he thought "cellar" sounded more dignified for this sort of place. He Googled it: A basement was a floor entirely or partly beneath ground level, while a cellar was small and meant for storing specific things, like wine or coal.

Only one way to find out.

But before that, he'd have to remove the stack of plastic storage containers barring it, which felt like a foreboding blockade. Nick wondered if this was his mom being superstitious. She was just as bad as Charlotte; she just didn't like to admit it. He moved them aside and tried to open it, but it was locked. There was an old-fashioned looking keyhole beneath the doorknob. He remembered the skeleton key in his coat pocket and grabbed it. The key slid awkwardly into the hole, and he had to jiggle it a bit, but it eventually clicked. Before turning the brass knob, he hesitated, dreading what he might find down there. It wasn't like he expected to find a monster. No, he feared something much worse, like mould or rats—real problems that he didn't know how to solve. He opened the door and, unsurprisingly, there was a staircase leading down into solid blackness. There was neither the noise of little feet scurrying nor the wet-socks stink of mould, so he turned on his phone's flashlight and walked down feeling optimistic. Moving his flashlight around the room, it seemed that it was pretty small, which was a point for the cellar category. However, he couldn't see any coal, wine bottles, or even firewood. He did notice a worktable and some shelves of books. There didn't seem to be a light fixture above him. Instead, there were a few candelabras holding what looked to be fresh candles. A box of new matches sat on the table. Nick lit the candles and the room soon became illuminated by a soft amber light.

The first thing he noticed was the carving on the table. It looked like a winged spider. Carved formations of webbing stretched out from it and across the table. On top of the table was a set of old glass beakers, scales, and tiny jars topped with cork stoppers. Nick had only done one chemistry course in high school, but he could tell this was more like something out of Professor Snape's potions class than Walter White's meth lab. Too bad Charlotte wasn't here; she'd love this shit. A leather-bound journal lay open on the table written in some language he didn't recognize. After studying Russian, Nick had an intermediary grasp of varying alphabets, but he couldn't place this one. The letters were more like hieroglyphs, crawling across the page like tiny little insects. The only things Nick could discern were the numbers at the header of the pages, which seemed to be dates, and the initials A.M. at the bottom. Alistair Moore? He found a couple more similar journals. There were also hardcover books on the shelves written in Greek, Latin, and more languages Nick didn't recognize. It seemed like Moore was into some kind of occult research and he wrote his thoughts in coded journals. He took one with him to show Charlotte. He also noticed a weird-looking rock on the table, too. It was round and smooth like a beach rock with two perfectly round holes bore through it. He held it up to his face like a pair of glasses from *The Flintstones*. Charlotte would probably get a kick out of that, too. Suddenly the idea of writing a book about Moore and his mansion felt a lot more exciting.

And this was totally a cellar.

When he came upstairs, Nick noticed a light was flashing near the main staircase. He approached it and it stopped. Another one at the top of the steps started flashing. He climbed the stairs and this one stopped too. The second floor was where most of the work needed to be done. This was where the guest rooms would go and there needed to be drywall put up, painting, and some work done on the floor. Before he could allow himself to feel too overwhelmed by all this, a light flickered at the top of the third floor. This was the old servants' quarters where his parents had initially set up their room. Before his father was confined to a hospital bed and it was more convenient to have it on the first floor.

This floor didn't have any of the fancy wainscotting or beadboards of the rest of the house. Nick could see the chandelier above him was a modern one his dad must have installed. At the back of the room was the shape of a tall floor mirror covered over with a blanket. Under the pulsating light, Nick could see Fred had repaired the damaged plaster walls. But there was a peculiar pattern on them. As he leaned closer to inspect it, the light suddenly stopped flickering and shone with a bright intensity. He could hear the electricity humming. Under this hard light, he could see the walls were streaked with white tendrils like a lightning storm. His first thought was mould, but this didn't look like any mould he'd ever seen before. Mould was spotty and kind of furry; this looked more like the neural network of a brain. Then again, he didn't know shit about any of this. He approached the mould to examine its texture. Up close, it looked like a tracing of dried salt. It reminded him of the bits of road salt that got on his boots or pants in winter. He noticed there were even tiny nodes scattered across the pattern. When he lifted his finger to touch it, the chandelier let out a kind of squeal then popped, sending shards of glass all over the room.

"Jesus Christ!" Nick screamed in fright and frustration.

He brushed the fine dust and fragmented glass from his arms, glad that there was no one around to have heard his shrill outburst. He grabbed a broom and dustpan and cleaned up. After another glance around the room, he realized he was going to need to hire a mould expert and contact whoever had done the electrical work. He checked his phone and was shocked to see it was past 3:30 pm. Somewhere along the line he'd lost an hour or two. How long had he been down in the cellar? He didn't have time to dwell on this because he had to rush back into town and pick up Charlotte. As he shuffled down the stairway towards the front door, he heard a sound that stopped him dead. It was like a sigh. More specifically, it sounded distinctly like the sigh his mother would make whenever he'd gotten on her last nerve. And, this was ridiculous, he felt her presence. Indeed, he felt her presence now more than he'd had whenever he'd come visit her over the last year while his dad was sick. Then she'd felt drained. But now it was like she was here, in her full essence. He took off his glasses and rubbed his eyes then ran his hands through his hair and massaged the back of his neck.

"This is fucking nuts," he muttered to himself, but quietly so as to not disturb anyone who may be nearby.

And then it—whatever it was—was gone.

He got into his car and decided there was no he way he could make up the thirty minutes of the two-hour drive without speeding like a maniac. He texted Charlotte to let her know she'd need to cab it. This gave him time to run a quick errand.

Nick stopped into the hardware and building supplies store in Northern Bay. The grey tile and grey paint on the walls were a far cry from the glossy aisles of Canadian Tire. The iron smell of nails and rubber boots filled the small store. He was greeted by a man wearing loose-fitting overalls.

"Howshegettingon," the man said in a swift, heavily accented flourish.

Nick smiled and nodded, unsure of what the man had said—also unsure whether this guy worked there or was just a local hanging out. He was about to speak when a short fiftyish-year-old man came in from the back lumber yard. He had a friendly smile that instantly de-aged him by about ten years.

"How can I help you?" the man asked with a north shore accent slightly less thick than the man in overalls.

"Hi," Nick answered, relieved. "I'm trying to renovate

an old house and it looks like I've got some mould issues. I was wondering if you could recommend someone to come have a look. I'll also need an electrician, too."

"Yes, I knows some people. Wher're y'located?"

"Up in Cachot Cove. Actually, it's the old merchant's mansion. Not sure if you're familiar with it."

Something changed behind the man's blue eyes.

"Yes, I'm familiar with it." His voice was stiff now, devoid of that previous friendliness.

"OK," Nick said. "Do you know anyone who could help me? And do you happen to know the electrician my parents hired?"

"I'll have to call around," the man said after hesitating. "Why don't you give me your number, and I'll get back to you."

Nick gave the man his cellphone number but felt like he was being given the same run around he'd experienced all too often on George Street with girls. That was all he could do at the moment, so he got back into his car and headed home. On the way, he decided that he'd earned some fried chicken and taters.

In their apartment, Charlotte lit some white candles, burned some sage, and laid out her protection crystals before daring to peruse Moore's journal. Nick detailed the day's events between mouthfuls of Mary Browns.

"That sounds like an alchemy set," Charlotte said after Nick described the equipment in the cellar. He was familiar with the term but didn't know much about it.

"What's alchemy for anyway?" he asked. "Turning lead into gold?"

"Chrysopoeia. Turning base metals into noble metals.

That's one part of alchemy. Other goals are creating a universal solvent and panaceas. Also, an elixir for immortality was big, too." She picked up the beach rock with the two holes in it.

"This is a hag stone, by the way," she explained. "It can be used for protections of all sorts. Also, if you look through the holes, you can see faeries."

"What about that book?"

"This is either a language Moore invented for himself or some kind of encryption that I'm not familiar with. You'd need the cipher to decrypt it."

She closed it and quickly laid it on the table like it was radioactive. Nick was disappointed by her lack of enthusiasm.

"I thought you'd find this stuff interesting."

"I do, but it seems like this guy was into some really black magic."

"Would you like to come have a look at the cellar sometime?"

"Maybe."

But Nick didn't think that sounded very promising. "What about your Ouija board?" he asked.

"What about it?"

"What if you asked your board about it, and, like, the spirits or whatever could tell you more about it."

Charlotte stared at Moore's journal like someone would with a dangerous, unpredictable animal. He could tell she was trying to formulate a way to explain this in plain language.

"Here's the thing," she started. "A Ouija board is used to communicate with your subconscious mind, not spirits.

It's called the ideomotor effect. Your body is moving without your conscious awareness. Like when you're asleep but reflexively move and wake up. It's a method to create or retrieve images from your subconscious. Believing spirits are moving the planchette is basically a placebo to enhance the ideomotor effect. It's also why it works better when multiple people have their hands on the planchette. Some researchers have actually used it with Alzheimer's patients to help with retrieving memories."

Nick subconsciously winced at the A-word.

"So why do you use it?" Nick asked.

"It's kind of like meditation. A way to check in with my subconscious. It's a powerful communication tool. But with yourself, not spirits." She yawned then and gave him a kiss. "I'm going to bed."

"I'm going to poke around at this for awhile longer," he said, pointing at the journal.

She went upstairs and Nick flicked through Moore's journal, trying in vain to make heads or tails of it. He fell into a series of Google rabbit holes, searching cryptography. Charlotte seemed to be correct to say they'd be lost without a cipher. He checked the time and saw that it was almost 3:30 am. It wasn't the first time he'd lost track of time researching random nonsense. But he didn't feel tired. Under the coffee table, he could see Charlotte's Ouija board. Quietly, he took it out. Charlotte was so fastidious with her crystals and sage and such that he was surprised to discover it was foam like a Monopoly board and the planchette was plastic; hardly the kind of prop you'd see in a movie. Then again, she did pretty much explain to him that she only really saw it as a meditation tool. He laid it out on the coffee table beside Moore's journal, then rested his hands on the planchette and thought about what he should ask it. Maybe he'd somehow manage to absorb some information about Moore and the mansion without remembering exact details. Or maybe Charlotte was wrong, and you really could communicate with spirits with this thing.

"How old is this book?"

He did his best to keep his hands and arms as relaxed as possible. Nothing happened for what felt like several minutes. He was about to bail when he felt his hands budge. Slowly, the planchette crept to the number 1 then 7 then 6. This journal was supposed to be 176 years old? That was impossible. Sure it was a little tattered, but it looked like something you could buy off the shelf in the Chapters' lifestyle section, one of those rustic journals writers bought and were afraid to write in. Charlotte was right; he wasn't communicating with spirits, only his own dumb brain.

Still, he wanted to ask more questions.

"What language is this journal written in?"

The planchette drifted towards A then M.

"Alistair Moore? He created the language?"

The planchette moved to the upper left corner beside a smiling sun: Yes.

"Is there a cipher?"

It moved to the upper right corner beside a haughty looking crescent moon: No.

Nick groaned. He leaned back on the sofa in frustration when the skin on the back of his neck prickled. The faint odour of salt water drifted to his nose. He could feel a familiar presence in the room with him. "Who am I speaking with?" he asked.

The planchette glided across the board: D-A-D.

The cheap plastic trembled between his shaking hands. It was all in his head, right?

"Where are you right now?"

His hands moved with a quicker and more deliberate pace, spelling out: C-A-C-H-O-T-C-O-V-E.

"No, you're in Carbonear."

No.

He licked his dry lips. His heart was thumping now. He did his best to disguise the tremor in his voice. "Was that really you who came here that night? Told me to stay away from the merchant's mansion?"

Yes.

"Is it dangerous there?"

Yes.

"Why?"

A-M.

"What about this journal? Is it safe?"

No.

Nick drew his hands back from the Ouija board like it was a burning stove. After some shaky breaths, he composed himself and laughed. The smell of salt water was gone. It was like Charlotte said, all in his head. His subconscious. That's what this whole thing has been about. Obviously, he's been through hell with his dad, and he had a deep desire to communicate with him, which manifested here on the board. And he's been stressed out about renovating the merchant's mansion, so his brain is telling him to stay away from it. And the journal being 176 years old? That's just his subconscious drawing on all that Gothic literature he's read. All perfectly rational. Nonetheless, before going to bed, he brought the journal out to his car.

* * *

"Well," the mould remediation guy said, "it's definitely not mould."

The streaks around the room seemed fainter now than they did the other day when Nick had first discovered them. They seemed more like thin spiderwebs as opposed to the lightning storm he'd remembered.

"Usually, in homes, the issue is black mould. And it starts in a part of the room, like a corner or under a sink, and spreads from there like a slimy rash. This isn't black and isn't spreading like mould normally would. The wallpaper isn't even peeling."

"So, what is it then?" Nick asked. He noticed buddy never actually touched the substance, whatever it was.

"I'd say someone drew it. Looks like chalk to me."

Nick thought about the mental state of not only his father but his mother as well, and it wasn't improbable that one of them had done it as some delusional fixation.

"I'll have a look around the house just to make sure nothing is wrong, but this place is nice and dry, so not a very mould-friendly place to grow."

Before Nick could tell him about the cellar, his phone buzzed with a number he didn't recognize.

"Hello, Nick speaking."

"Hi, my name is Brian Johnston. I did the electrical work in your parents' place."

"Yeah, thanks for getting back to me. I'm having some

issues with the lights. A chandelier actually exploded. I was wondering if you could come have a look."

"Unfortunately, I can't come out."

"Oh?"

"My back is bad."

Nick was unconvinced.

"Well, what am I supposed to do? I don't want to have to pay another electrician to fix this. I shouldn't have to."

"I apologize. I'll reimburse you for whatever costs."

"How do I know you're not going to screw me over?"

"Just give me your email and I'll transfer you the money. I'm really sorry, but I just can't go back in that house."

After Nick gave him his email, Brian promptly ended the call.

"Alright," the mould guy called out. "All done."

Nick met him at the door. The guy seemed eager to leave.

"Sorry for wasting your time," Nick said. "How much do I owe you?"

"Don't worry about it."

"Are you sure?"

"Yeah. I heard about your folks. I was sorry to hear that."

"Thanks, I appreciate it."

The guy got back into his truck then paused.

"Can I tell you something?" he said. "You're probably going to think I'm half-cracked, though."

"Go ahead."

"That house gives me the creeps."

"The cellar is pretty freaky. I think the old owner was

into some paranormal kind of stuff."

"It's not just that. I don't know what it is, but it feels unnatural."

"How so?"

"Like it's too preserved. A house that old that's been left alone that long should have all kinds of issues with it, but except for having to get it up to modern code, it's just a bit of wear and tear. Not even the mice will go handy to it. Just creeps me s'all."

They said their goodbyes and Nick went back inside to turn off the lights. He wanted to leave early today so he could visit his parents. As he passed through the third floor, he noticed the streams seemed different. They were definitely thicker than when the mould guy was here and looked more like what he'd remembered the first time he'd come across them. The patterns were changed, too. He took out his phone and snapped a picture then hurried out of the house to make his way to Carbonear.

At the hospital, Olivia lay in her bed, watching the television with her lids barely open. Nick sat beside her. It was some TLC show about renovating a house, which was the last thing he wanted to watch at the moment so he changed the channel to Sportsnet. Of course, it was a crew of talking heads bleating about the Toronto Maple Leafs and their race to the bottom for Auston Matthews.

"The Habs should be trying harder to tank," Nick said to his mom, who barely seemed to register he was there. "Really goes to show how much Price was bailing them out. Whatever they do, they better not trade Subban."

Nick wondered how much of this was getting through. Despite the doctor's early enthusiasm, his mom had plateaued these last few weeks. She was often very lethargic and didn't speak much. Whenever he visited, he liked to just ramble on in the hopes that some part of her registered this interaction and kept her moored to reality.

"I picked up where you and dad left off with the old merchant's mansion," he said. "I was in the attic where you guys had set up your bedroom and noticed some weird streaks on the walls, like they'd been drawn with chalk or something. Did you or dad do that?"

He looked down at his mom and saw that her eyes were now wide open. She stared at him with a frightening intensity.

"Luh...luh...luh...heave," she croaked.

"You want me to go?" Nick stood up, afraid that he was making her confused and anxious somehow.

She shook her head.

"Ha...ha...how...suh."

"Leave the house? You mean the mansion?"

She nodded then sank back down to the pillow. Tears rolled down her cheeks. Not wanting to cause her any more stress, Nick left. He got in his car and contemplated calling Alison, but he knew what she'd say. That the house had been a huge source of stress for her and was a bad association. Nick made a mental note not to bring it up whenever he visited. Before he pulled out of the parking lot, his phone buzzed. It was an email. Brian Johnston had sent him an e-transfer for $30,000.

* * *

Olivia was lost in time.

She couldn't remember the last time she'd spoke with

the doctor or one of the nurses. The pain in her stomach was setting her body on fire. She was pressing the button the nurse had given her, but no one was coming. Her bed was wet, wet with her blood. She looked down over the small bump in her stomach and could see the white sheets sodden red. The baby wasn't due for about another two months, so something was terribly wrong. She kept pushing the button. No one came. Maybe it was broken.

"Help!" she cried out. Or tried to. A raspy pharyngeal *hhhhh* was all she could manage.

She realized that unless she got out of bed and found a nurse she was going to bleed to death. Using her arms to push her torso up, the pain intensified. Any kind of bending in her midsection sent her nervous system into mayhem. She took a couple breaths, readying herself to swing her legs over. It was going to hurt; it might even knock her out. With one swift motion, she swung her legs over the side of the bed. Her body trembled with pain. She grabbed the IV stand beside her to steady herself. The bed shook wildly as she shuddered. The pain wouldn't retreat. It was the sitting position, too much pressure on her stomach. With two hands she seized the IV stand and drove herself up. Her legs wobbled, weak and unsteady like a toddler as she made her way into the hall.

There were no nurses to be found, so she started wandering, pleading with her soundless voice. Looking in the rooms, she saw grey-haired, wrinkly people lying in beds. Wasn't this the maternity ward? She looked back and saw a trail of blood leading to her room. Her vision narrowed into a dark tunnel, the world receding into a blurring soup. If she didn't get help soon, she was going to collapse here on the floor and bleed to death.

That's when she heard the familiar voice of a young man coming from a nearby room. Perhaps it was her doctor. It was a big room divided into two sections. To the left were a couple couches and to the right was a hospital bed. This must be the delivery room, where the father can wait on the couch while the mother gave birth. She saw Fred to the right talking to a young man who she didn't recognize. She saw herself lying in the bed, asleep and pale, like she was dead.

"We can't stop the bleeding," the young man said. "We're going to have to perform a hysterectomy."

"Was it a boy or girl?" Fred asked.

"A boy," the doctor said.

But the doctor was her son, Nicholas. She knew he could've been a doctor or a lawyer or anything he wanted to be if he'd only set his mind to something. The mistake was buying him that damn guitar when he was thirteen. Everything after that went out the window, hockey, school. All he wanted to do was play that awful music with his new friends. They were a bad influence as far as she was concerned—got him into the drugs. If only she could make him see that she wanted the best for him. Alison had been so much easier.

"I think he turned out OK," Fred said.

"Yes," Olivia sighed. "I know. He just frustrates the hell out of me."

Fred smiled. He knew all about it.

He came up from behind her and kissed her cheek. Together they looked out over Cachot Cove harbour from their kitchen window. Gulls circled in the cloudless sky above a calm, blue ocean.

"Should be a grand day out in the boat," she said.

"Thanks for breakfast, dear," he said and was out the door.

She looked down at the plate in her hand and saw blood pouring from the faucet. The plate fell from her hands and shattered on the floor. Her apron was soaked red, and her hands were sticky with blood. She tried to scream, but all that came out was a hoarse pharyngeal *hh-hhh*.

CHAPTER FIVE

A friendly face greeted Nick shortly after he rang the bell. The man held the door wide open and stood to the side to make room for Nick to enter.

"Hi, my name is Nick O'Keefe. I just bought the merchant's mansion."

"Hello," the man said and re-positioned himself to block the entrance, his friendly demeanour instantly faltering.

"I'm curious about the history of the house and was wondering if you'd be able to share any stories you have."

"No, sorry," the man answered too quickly. "It's been empty for as long as I've been around. That's all I know about it." He spoke low as if he was afraid someone was listening, gently pulling the door shut.

"OK," Nick said, not wanting to push the issue. "Well, thanks for your time."

The man nodded and promptly shut his door. In his yard, a pygmy goat emerged from a tiny little barn with the words "Cans" painted above the entrance. Two horns like big bananas crowned its head. The goat bleated angrily at Nick, as if to say it didn't want him around either.

With the exception of the goat, this pattern continued for the rest of the houses he visited. People either professed to know nothing about the mansion or were suddenly very busy and needed to be somewhere, which Nick found odd considering the fish plant was closed for the season and most of the town were either unemployed or retired. He knocked on every door on the Protestant side, working his way systematically from the merchant's mansion towards the centre of town. Before starting in on the Catholics, he decided he'd earned an Orange Crush and a bag of Doritos. As he walked towards the town's store, an old woman exited with a reusable bag in each hand. Nick recognized her as the lady who'd called the ambulance for his mom. Inside, he grabbed his junk food while the woman working did her best to pretend she wasn't staring at his tattoos.

"Excuse me," Nick asked. "Would you mind telling me the name of the woman who was just in here before me."

"That's Agnes Noonan," she answered, then added unprompted: "She lives on Blundon Lane. Number five."

"Thanks."

The woman nodded like she'd anticipated giving this information long in advance. Of course, word must have gotten around Cachot Cove about what had happened to his parents. Nick also supposed word would soon get around that he was asking about the mansion. That likely meant more pre-rehearsed excuses and feigned ignorance. At least he now had a strong lead in the Catholic side of town.

Checking Google Maps, Nick found Ms. Noonan's house on the southern end part of Cachot Cove, just about the opposite side as Moore's mansion. There was no way this old woman could have looked across town in the middle of the night and saw his mom having a stroke, even if she'd been perfectly framed in the window like a Hitchcock movie. He formulated a plan of attack as he sat on a bench digging his way through his chips. She wasn't going to shut him out like the rest of this town. After throwing away his trash, he walked to her house and knocked. The door opened after a brief wait, revealing the diminutive old woman.

"I was wondering if you were going to come," Ms. Noonan said. "Come in."

She showed Nick to a table in her living room. He sat down and she poured him a cup of tea without asking if he'd wanted one. On the wall were pictures of what Nick guessed were her children, grandchildren, and maybe even great-grandchildren.

"I saw you walking around, so I boiled the kettle," she explained.

Nick felt bad now for having prepared himself to give her the third degree. Clearly, she had something to say about the house and was eager to share.

"My name is Nick O'Keefe—" he began.

"I suppose you wants to know about the house you bought, is it?"

"Yes."

"Well, I was the last person to work there before Mr. Moore died, so I'd be the best person to ask."

Nick couldn't believe his luck.

"Ms. Noonan—" he started.

"Agnes is fine."

"Agnes, I get the sense that people are almost scared of the house. Why is that?"

"People think the house is unnatural. And they thought the same of Mr. Moore, too. I took the job when I was a young woman to support my family. My husband had died in a fishing accident and left me with four children, so we were desperate. This was before Confederation, mind you. If things got bad back then you didn't have government to help you out. People starved."

"I'm sorry to hear about your husband," Nick offered.

Agnes sipped her tea and didn't respond.

"What do you mean by 'unnatural?'" he continued.

She smiled. "You've been in there. I'm sure I don't have to tell you."

She was right. Nick knew what she meant. There was no other word to describe it. The house didn't abide the laws of atrophy, like it was following its own separate speed on time's arrow. Not to mention whatever was going on with the lights.

"What about Mr. Moore?"

"He's a different story," Agnes said after a long sip of tea. "When I started working there, he was very old, but no one could rightly say how old. He'd outlived all his family members and he didn't have any children. I must say, if it weren't for the queer feeling I got in the house, it was a very easy job. Mice stayed away; dust didn't seem to settle much at all. And my day always went by rather quickly even though I wasn't busy. The only issue were the bugs.

Lots of those. Most of the job was feeding and cleaning up after Mr. Moore. At that point he was just about dead to the world. I'd change his clothes, give him bed baths, and clean his business, and he never paid me no mind. He just stared off in the distance like he was watching something that only he could see."

That sounded all too familiar to Nick.

"Is that it?" he asked. "Seems a little out of proportion to how people react to it."

"You see, there was a rumour that Mr. Moore was keen on the supernatural, black magic, witchcraft."

"I see."

"That's how people account for his long life and the state of the house."

"Do you know what sort of things he was doing?"

"Mind you, I never saw any of it myself, but I heard plenty of stories. People said he had bookcases full of rare and odd books written in strange languages no one could read. He must have gotten rid of them by the time I arrived, or someone else did."

Nick thought about what he'd found in the cellar. Maybe Moore had tried to cover his tracks later in life and those were the last of his collection that he couldn't bear to part with. He made a mental note to go down there again and take a closer look at them.

"Any kind of rituals?" Nick asked.

"People talked about seeing him in the windows with candles lit all hours of the night. Other people talked about him going into the woods to commune with the fay."

"Faeries?"

Agnes nodded and sipped her tea.

"Mostly, people talked about the black ledger he kept," she continued. "Back then, merchants controlled everything. They tracked how much cod you caught, what they sold it for, and then counted what you earned versus what you borrowed from them. You see, before Confederation, most Newfoundlanders didn't carry cash, it was all on the 'truck' system as they called it. Just about the only way to get a few coppers for yourself was the seal hunt. Besides that, you relied on the merchant for your groceries, building supplies, wood, fishing gear, everything! It was a travesty really. And, of course, many of the merchants took advantage because Newfoundlanders could barely read or write, so they had to trust what the merchant told them. Luckily, Mr. Moore was generous compared to some of the merchants in other outports. He made sure families were looked after during the winter months or if the catch had been bad that season or if the cod weren't selling well. But you had to sign your name in the black ledger."

"What was that?" He couldn't remember seeing anything like that in the cellar.

"A separate book he kept. It was like a contract. That if you signed your name, he'd make sure you and your family were taken care of. Most were quick to sign. After all, it was just a signature. Or an X if you couldn't write your name. But then people started saying it was a contract for your soul. Most dismissed it as some silly thing from an eccentric man, but as he got older, and the house gained its reputation, people began to wonder how silly it really was. I'll tell you something else, the ones who signed those contracts started going funny in their heads before their time."

"Like senile? Dementia?"

"Yes, I believe that's what they calls it now."

"What do you think?"

Agnes shrugged her shoulders. "Maybe it is just a bunch of nonsense. People often make up in their head something is so, then look for reasons to show they're right but ignore whatever makes them wrong. Do you know what I mean?"

Nick nodded. The fancy term for that was "confirmation bias."

"Yes. Maybe that's all it is. But you know what? I'm over ninety years myself and aside from a bit of arthritis on cold days like this, I don't feel one bit old. I get the cold shoulder around here because people think Mr. Moore used some of his magic on me for good service. I can tell you right now that's not true because that man never spoke a word the ten years I worked there until I found him dead in his bed one morning."

Nick looked down and realized that he'd been so rapt he'd neglected his tea. The bag had sunk to the bottom of the black brew. He took two lukewarm astringent mouthfuls then decided it was time to ask the question he'd really wanted to ask since coming here.

"Agnes," he said, "how did you know my mom was in trouble?"

She gave him a hard look. He started to worry she wasn't going to answer him or maybe even kick him out.

"I felt it," she said.

Nick raised an eyebrow.

"I woke up in the middle of the night and somehow I

just knew your parents were in trouble over there. Tell the truth and shame the devil. I had a bad feeling ever since they first bought the place and moved in. It's like I can feel it in my gut when someone is in there, moving around in there."

Nick took another sip of tepid, strong tea and swallowed hard, unsure what to say.

"If you want some advice, love," Agnes continued, "get out. Do whatever you need to do and be rid of it. And don't look back."

"Thanks for the tea," he said and stood up.

He was almost out the door when Agnes spoke up again.

"And stay away from those woods," she said. "No one goes handy to them."

Nick thanked her again and headed back to the mansion, a fresh layer of anxiety burning in his belly. On the way he started doing some math. Moore had died in 1949. Agnes said she took care of him for ten years after her husband died to support her young family. People married much younger back then, but it wasn't like there were child brides. Nick supposed she was likely sixteen when she married then had four kids. That would take at least three years, which would put her at around twenty when she started working. So, by the time Moore died sixty-seven years ago, she was thirty. That would put her at ninety-seven now. He wondered how many people that age lived alone and could make regular trips to the store. Even if he'd added a few years in his estimation, that was still remarkable. Maybe Moore had really gifted her long life.

He was resolved now to get these renovations done as

quickly as possible. With the money he'd gotten from the electrician, he could just hire some guys to come in and finish just about whatever else needed done. Then he'd be done with it. He'd sell the house and use the profit to live off and focus on his writing.

Before he opened the door, he felt something graze the back of his neck. It felt like a whisper.

Help.

He turned around but there was nothing there. Just the wind blowing through the small copse. Still, he couldn't help feeling like the woods were calling out to him. Slowly, he walked towards the tree line. It was only a small grove, but the bramble was too thick to see through to the other side. He noticed there was what appeared to be a footpath leading into the woods, but the trail was blocked by tightly entangled limbs. Likely the route Moore used to take during his excursions, long since grown over. A strong wind bristled the branches again. "Psithurism." That's what it was. People used to think they heard voices in the woods, believing it to be faeries or whatever, but really it was the wind rustling the leaves. The brain will often anthropomorphize natural phenomena, like seeing a face in a cliffside when it's just a bunch of rocks. Nick turned when he heard it again.

Help.

This time the wind switched directions, pushing him towards the woods. The patch of thistle seemed to part, opening a passage for him.

HELP!

This knocked him backwards and he stumbled towards the house, not taking his eyes off the woods.

Inside, he took a deep breath then laughed at himself. He could imagine Charlotte with a face full of "told you so." Spirits, faeries, black magic—once you accepted these things were true it was easy to start interpreting stuff to fit the narrative. Like Agnes had said, confirmation bias. That could be an interesting angle for his book. A house became haunted not by ghosts but by the narratives that were heaped upon it. He gave his head a shake and made his way to the kitchen. He paused before the cellar door, suddenly anxious again. After a deep breath he opened it and shuffled downstairs with his cell's flashlight. It took a couple trips, but he managed to collect all the books and journals. There were professors in the Linguistics and Classics departments at the university he could show those books. They might even be valuable. But there was no sign of that black ledger Agnes had described. By the time he was finished that, it was almost 3 pm. Before leaving, he decided he'd take a sweep of the house to see if the lights were acting up again.

Everything seemed fine, so he decided to replace the lights in the third-floor chandelier. He switched on the new bulbs, illuminating the strange patterns on the walls. Fed up looking at them, he filled up a bucket with water and soap and returned with a sponge. The streaks seemed to throb like blood pulsing through veins. Nick took a step forward to get a closer look. Not watching where he was going, he barked his knee off a nightstand. Something rolled inside it. He pulled the drawer out and saw half a dozen sticks of chalk. The mould guy had said the streaks looked like something someone had drawn. Nick imagined his father drawing all this in the midst of some manic delusion. His mom had likely been too burnt out to try and stop him or clean it up.

But then something beside the chalk sent chills through his body. A black ledger. It was long and rectangular and looked almost like a guest book. Unlike the other books he'd found here, this one was actually all English. It was filled with names, dates, and signatures, starting at 1849. This must have been Moore's old ledger where he kept track of credit he loaned the fishermen. But there were no dollar totals anywhere. Also, didn't his parents say that Moore died shortly after Confederation? That was 1949. Moore would have to be at least the age of an adult before he could run Cachot Cove's fishery. That would mean he'd been at least 120 when he died. No, that didn't make sense. Maybe he'd inherited this from his father. But there was "A.M." initialled beside the signatures all over the pages from the beginning. Maybe they had the same name or initials. Nick continued to leaf through the book until he got to the last page. He noticed another strange thing: the ink wasn't faded. The signatures from the mid-nineteenth century were as clear and bold as something written with a modern BIC ballpoint. Then he got to the last page and nearly dropped it from the shock of what he saw. The last two signatures were his parents'. Nick stared at it, over-whelmed by the unreality. Sure enough. There was Glen Blunden, February 26, 1936, then Fred O'Keefe, October 27, 2014. That was about a year and a half ago, around the time his dad started showing signs of dementia. Then, beneath Fred's name was Olivia's. November 3, 2015. Not even a year ago. Around which time he noticed her acting strangely as well. But what really unsettled Nick were the initials "A.M." beside their signatures. He shut the book and dropped it on the table with a thud. Time to clean all this shit up.

The lights began flickering and its electric hum rose in pitch the closer he got to the streaks with the sponge. He dropped the sponge in the bucket and the frequency dropped from a Rob Halford screech to unnoticeable hertz. The streaks now seemed to be pulsating like exposed nerves. He looked closely and saw a gentle rise and fall like the foam from a wave's crest. The hum returned now, but this time it was a gentle croon. Nick licked his lips and tasted the faint flavour of salt like he'd just had some chips. The streaks twisted and writhed until they formed a steady pattern that seemed to emanate from the covered mirror. He removed the sheet and saw a cracked mirror framed by wrought black iron. A fissure in the middle rippled outwards like a spider web from the mirror and onto the walls. Nick was transfixed. As he stared, the lines began to quiver like veins, throbbing in time with his own heartbeat. He didn't notice the drool trickling from his mouth. It was hypnotizing to behold, and he dared not blink even though his eyes had become red and dry.

The low, gentle hum lulled him to the point that he barely registered the pattern creeping towards him, fractalizing into patterns inside patterns. They expanded and shrunk into bundles of nerves, spiderwebs, octopus tentacles, cauliflower, seashells, snowflakes, and finally a shoreline, which rushed towards him. Nick felt like he was now falling from the sky and was about to strike the earth. He shut his eyes and screamed.

When he opened them, he found himself lying on a

carpet. He stood up and looked around. To his sides were tall stone pillars and in front of him was a dais leading to a throne. Behind the throne was a tall slim window bathing the room in brilliant light. Nick wondered how he'd managed to find himself on the set of *Game of Thrones*. As his eyes adjusted, he realized someone was sitting atop the throne.

"Nicholas O'Keefe," a deep voice boomed all around him. "Welcome."

"Uhh…hello…" Nick managed after some effort.

"You're probably wondering where you are and how you got here." The voice was now localized to the individual sitting in the chair. He rose and walked down the dais towards Nick, holding out a hand. Nick took it and immediately felt the strength behind it as he rose from his knees. The man smiled. He reminded Nick of Golden Age Hollywood actors like Kirk Douglas as Spartacus. But there was something off about it, something uncanny. Like his face was actually a really exceptional computer-generated image of a classically handsome man but unable to fully render that ineffable human quality.

"My name is Alistair Moore," he said. "But perhaps you already knew that."

"Pleased to meet you," Nick replied, now fully realizing he was dreaming.

"I know you're an intelligent young man, so I'll cut to the chase. You are still in Cachot Cove," More pronounced it *cash-oh* with the proper French enunciation, "but you're in a far better version. My version." Moore noticed the incredulous look on Nick's face. "You probably think you're dreaming, but I assure you that's not the case. Come, look."

He guided Nick to the window behind the throne. Together they looked out upon a sun-drenched Cachot Cove. Except the concrete government wharf and fish plant were replaced by rickety wooden fishing stages. Vinyl-sided houses were replaced by wooden biscuit and saltboxes. It was like Nick had gone back in time.

"Would you like to see it?"

"Sure," Nick replied, unsure what else to say.

Moore lay an arm on Nick's shoulders and guided him out of the room. Tall, arched hallways extended from both sides. Tapestries adorned the walls and the rug underneath his feet was gentler than any carpet he'd ever walked on. Long, interlocking Celtic knots were stitched into the fabrics. Sections of the walls were interrupted by tall stained-glass windows filling the hallway in shimmering light. They depicted images of fishermen hauling nets of fish from the water and presenting their catch to a benevolent figure. Nick felt like he was walking inside an aquarium.

Moore led Nick into the dining hall. A long wooden table stretched the length of the room beside an unlit firepit carved into the wall. Some women dressed in old-fashioned aprons emerged from a back room, which Nick assumed was the kitchen. They carried buckets of vegetables, meats, and salt, keeping their eyes down when they saw Moore. Nick recognized the walking gait of one of the women.

"Mom?" he asked.

Olivia stopped and turned. She looked to be in her late twenties, not much older than Nick, but he still recognized her. There was a brief moment of panic in her expression before she turned her eyes down.

"Hello, Nicholas," she said.

"I'm afraid we don't have time for much of a reunion at the moment," Moore said, his hand resting firmly on Nick's shoulder. "But all in due course."

He again guided Nick away with that gentle firmness. Completely bewildered by what was happening, Nick simply went with the flow. The rest of the castle's details were a blur and the next thing he knew he was outside in the warm summer air, fresh and clean, devoid of exhaust fumes. Instead of the sound of cars, he heard men's voices from the wharf and gulls screeching overhead. He felt the sun's warmth, which was softened by a gentle ocean breeze carrying its briny fragrance.

They made their way on the rutted path towards the wharf. Nick recognized that the castle was overlooking this dreamlike Cachot Cove in the same position as the merchant's mansion. Weathered, tanned men in wool guernseys eyed Nick with curiosity but looked away when Moore turned his attention to them.

"Nicholas?" a familiar voice called out.

Nick looked to one of the fishing stages and saw his father. "Dad?"

They ran to each other and embraced. Like Olivia, Fred was his younger self, like an old photograph come to life. Fred opened his mouth to speak then looked to Moore. He stepped back and nodded.

"I was just showing young Nicholas around," Moore explained. "My apologies for not indulging this further, but time is limited as you understand."

Fred nodded again and returned to his work. Men and women scurried about on fish flakes like busy ants, inspecting drying filleted cod, liberally tossing handfuls of salt. The flakes stood atop wooden beams where more people hauled fish and buckets of salt. Out in the harbour, boats were docking beside stages built into the rocky coastline, unloading the day's catch. The boats were loaded down to the gunnels with the weight of the fish, barely keeping above water. It reminded Nick of the set of *Waterworld*.

"Impressive," Alistair Moore said smugly, "isn't it?"

Before Nick could reply, he was being guided back to the castle. He tried to look back to see his dad again, but he was lost amidst the hustle and bustle of the harbour. If this were a lucid dream, shouldn't he be able to control what was happening? Or force himself awake? He certainly had that surreal, out-of-body feeling, but when he pushed his consciousness to wake, he felt himself run up against some kind of psychic wall.

Moore led Nick to a massive library, with rows of shelves stretching to the ceiling, filled with books. They sat at a long table. "Your parents tell me you're a bit of an academic," Moore said.

Nick didn't answer; he just kept looking through the titles.

"I devoted my life to learning," Moore continued. "I read the ancient Greek and Roman masters. Plato, Aristotle, Seneca. My father criticized me for being more interested in ideas than business. Nonetheless, he paid for my education—even sent me to Oxford. So, I must thank him for that. Of course, this was on the understanding that I take over the family trade. That was fine. I'd run the fishery in Cachot Cove and continue my reading in my own time. But we disagreed on how to run things. My father was a hard man, you see. I see a bit of him in Fred if I may say so." Nick couldn't argue with that. "He demanded all accounts be settled each season. And if a fisherman didn't make back what he owed, then he wasn't allowed to borrow until he paid back his debt next season. People starved. Father said if he indulged them, they wouldn't work hard, wouldn't respect him. I saw things differently. I believed that if you cared for people and took care of them, they would reward you."

"Is this where your black ledger comes in?" Nick asked. "People signed away their souls for some extra rations in the winter?"

Moore laughed. "That's a very melodramatic way of putting it. I can see you'd make an excellent author of fiction. Yes, there was a kind of psychical exchange. I learned about this magic through my studies. To live beyond death. And as you can see, I've built a paradise! Surely this is preferable to the ineffable void that awaits us?"

Moore slid that ledger across the table to Nick.

"You want me to sign this so I wind up like my parents? Like vegetables?"

"I had no doing with what happened to your parents. My understanding is that the science behind this Alzheimer's is still developing in your crude world."

Nick considered it. Yes, Fred's dementia and Olivia's stroke were jarring but were perfectly explainable by modern science. Alzheimer's was on the rise, and younger men than Fred were being diagnosed. And anyone can have a stroke, especially someone as burnt out as Olivia, sad to say.

"I could use someone like yourself here, to help with my research," Moore continued. "Look around. You could spend several lifetimes here in my library. Imagine if you had the chance to visit the Library of Alexandria. That's what I'm offering you. You'd have time to learn Greek, Latin, all the Romance languages. Read the great works in their original."

Nick looked around. It seemed like each direction he turned the stacks extended further. He thought about his life back in the real world. What was there for him? No job, a shitty apartment, a writing career going nowhere, and a bitch of a home improvement project. And Charlotte? Well, if she didn't want to join him, he saw some attractive women down at the harbour. And his parents were here too. Maybe he could finally have the sensible, adult relationship with them he'd always wanted.

He stared at the paper and pen sitting on the desk a little longer, still unable to make up his mind, when a thought occurred to him: he could outfox this Alistair Moore. While he played the role of assistant, he'd learn Moore's magic and use it against him. That would show them what he was capable of, show his parents and sister he wasn't the screw up they thought he was.

He signed, not seeing the grin on Moore's face.

* * *

Nick was lost in time.

"What do you mean you're quitting?" Fred demanded, lying in his hospital bed.

"What do you think I mean? I mean I'm done," Nick replied.

"Why?" Olivia asked, she was getting the bowls and sponges ready for Fred's bath.

"I just am. I don't want to play anymore."

"Do you have any idea how much money we've spent on your hockey?" Fred said.

"I don't care," Nick replied. "I didn't ask you to spend that money."

"Just give us a reason," Olivia said.

Nick could never help falling for their good cop/bad cop routine.

"Because you guys put too much pressure on me," Nick said. "It's not fun anymore."

"Life isn't always supposed to be fun," Fred said.

Olivia removed Fred's blanket to reveal his stained sheets. Nick had to turn his head.

"Yeah, well it isn't always supposed to be miserable either," Nick countered.

"Ever since we got you a guitar, all you want to do is play in that band with your new friends," Fred said. "Everything else has gone down the drain. Maybe we should just take it away."

Nick felt the temperature of his blood rise. "It's the only thing I can do without you two being up my hole!"

"Maybe you'd prefer it if we were the type of parents who didn't care what you did?" Olivia said, changing Fred's diaper. "Just let you drift through life, never make anything of yourself?"

"That sounds pretty nice, actually," Nick answered.

He turned around and stomped up the stairway before his parents could respond. These sorts of arguments could go fourteen rounds, and he knew his parents had more endurance than he did, so they'd eventually wear him down until he submitted to their will. He was sick of them throwing their money in his face with their unrequited labours of love. *We do all this for you, we spend all this money on you, now you have to do what we say!* He was only fifteen, what choice did he have? It's not like he could drop out of school, get a job, and set out on his own. Besides, it was never enough. If he gave in on hockey, then after that it would be his grades, then it would be volunteering somewhere to boost his resume, then something else, something else, something else. It never ended. Better to stick his flag somewhere and hold the line.

He wished Alison was around. At least then he wouldn't be outnumbered. But he knew now that wasn't true, didn't he? She would take their parents' side, albeit more diplomatically. She'd say, "Oh, that's just the way they are. Go along to get along." What about the way he was? Why didn't they go along with him to get along with him? Why was he always the one to compromise? Why was he always the one outnumbered 3-1? But he knew the answer to that, too, didn't he? He wasn't part of the circle. Of course, if he were to ever sneak into their bedrooms at night and shake them awake and say, "Am I really a part of this family?!" They'd say, "Yes, yes, why would you think otherwise?" But it was in the blood, somewhere hidden from the conscious mind—blood he didn't share. And that's what it came down to.

He dipped his brush in the can of paint and got to work on a wall. The steady, monotonous work allowed his mind to drift away from the argument. He thought about what it would be like to finally sell the merchant's mansion and be rid of it, free of this obligation to his family. Maybe he'd move to Vancouver or Montreal. Just get away, start again somewhere new.

A pair of arms wrapped around his waist and he felt a kiss on his neck. The hands unbuttoned his shirt and rubbed his stomach. All the hard work on the merchant's mansion had melted the spare tire and his abs showed through again. The hands drifted down towards and undid his belt. He turned around and found a young woman who wasn't Charlotte.

"What's wrong?" she asked.

Nick stepped back. "Who are you?"

She laughed. "I'm your wife, stunned ass."

He looked around. This wasn't his room. It wasn't the merchant's mansion. Unsure what to say, he just stared at her.

"Moore promised you to me," she said with her hands on her hips.

"Moore?" Nick repeated.

"Do you have any idea how long I've been waiting here all alone? I'm the only spinster of all of Cachot Cove." She started quietly sobbing

"I'm sorry," Nick said. "I think there's been some kind of confusion."

He stepped towards her, and when she looked up, bright lights shone from her eyes, blinding Nick. A car horn wailed. He swerved the car back into his lane as the car passed him by, still blasting the horn. It was dark, but he didn't have to see to know what finger the driver was holding up through the window. He pulled over to the side of the road and rolled down the window. Cold wind and rain rebooted his senses. He looked around and saw that he was in St. John's. Empire Avenue. Only a few minutes away from his apartment. He must have fallen asleep at the wheel. Working too hard. He got back onto the road and made his way to his apartment.

"Where the hell have you been?" Charlotte demanded as Nick entered the door.

"Huh?" he replied.

"I haven't heard from you in days besides the odd text."

Nick closed the door and took off his shoes. He felt exhausted but wasn't sure why. The last few days he'd been very busy at the merchant's mansion—working on what exactly? Plastering, drywall, tiling: there was so much work to be done it all just started to blur together. He brushed past Charlotte and went to the kitchen to retrieve a beer from the fridge. It was too tiring to speak or even think.

"Well?" Charlotte asked.

"Well what?" Nick answered and plopped on the couch, looking through Netflix to see what he'd like to watch while he vegged out.

"What do you have to say for yourself?"

"Can we talk about this later? I'm wiped."

Charlotte grunted and stomped up the stairs. Nick heard the bedroom door slam. He turned on *The Office* and took a long sip of beer. The lager was smooth and crisp. Its mellow glow quickly replaced the throbbing pain in his head. He sunk deeper into the couch. The image on the TV blurred and his eyelids became too heavy to keep open.

When he opened them, he found himself in a small wooden boat at sea. He looked around, confused and slightly panicked. But the waves were too gentle to cause anxiety. Across from him sat his father, tending to the oars.

"Beautiful day," Fred said.

"Yeah," Nick replied, then saw the sadness behind his father's eyes. "What's wrong?"

Fred looked up at the sky. "Oh nothing."

Nick looked up and saw a murder circling above them. Strange to see crows out this far. Maybe they were just really dark gulls. He noticed, too, that they were slight and skinny in the middle with large wings that flapped so quickly it was hard to distinguish them; they floated with a mechanic, almost insectile motion, like drones.

"Let's just enjoy this day together," Fred said.

He reached into a bucket of squid and attached one to the hook of a handline then handed it to Nick.

"Toss 'er over," he explained. Nick did as he was told. "Now, jiggle it to get their attention."

Again, Nick did as he was told. It didn't take long for him to feel a tug.

"Now," Fred said, "pull hard."

Nick pulled sharply on the landline and was surprised by how quickly the opposing force relinquished its struggle. Hand over hand, he drew up the codfish. It was about the length of his arm and must have weighed nearly eighty pounds.

"That's a beauty," Fred exclaimed. He came over with

a knife and slit the fish's gills to release the hook then tossed the cod into the centre of the boat.

"So that's cod jigging?" Nick remarked. Fred smiled and baited another hook.

They repeated this over and over until the boat was in danger of sinking from the weight of their catch. The sun burned the salty sweat on Nick's forehead. No number of deadlifts could have matched the workout he'd just given his lower back. But instead of feeling tired, the labour had him feeling energized. They rowed the mile or two back to shore. Olivia was waiting for them at the stage. Fred unloaded the fish from the boat onto the platform using a pike, forking the fish out of the boat like piles of hay. Inside the shed, Olivia showed Nick how to cut the codfish across the throat and down the belly. After he'd hand her a sliced fish, she'd remove the liver and toss it into a bucket. She then decapitated and gutted the cod, dropping the head and guts through a hole down into the water where eager gulls awaited, snapping up their supper.

As they made their way through the day's catch, Nick was occasionally struck by the absurdity of the situation. What the hell were they all doing playing out these roles from some nineteenth century pageant? But he was afraid to express these thoughts out of fear he might shatter this fragile dream. Even more, he was happy that they'd seemingly abandoned their incessant need to correct and micromanage.

With the day's work over, they made their way to Fred and Olivia's house, a tidy pink biscuit box in the centre of Cachot Cove.

"Oh my Jesus Christ!" Olivia shouted when they were

inside, releasing energy she'd been storing all afternoon. Nick was confused.

Fred shut and locked the door. "What the hell are you doing here?" he said to Nick.

"What do you mean?" Nick replied. "I fell asleep on my couch and next thing I knew I was in the boat."

"No. Earlier when you were out with Moore. You travelled here from the mirror in the attic, didn't you?"

Nick scratched his head. "Yeah, I think that's how it happened."

"I told you not to come after us. It's dangerous."

"Did you sign the book?" Fred asked.

Nick had to think about that. He'd lost track of the last few days. But focusing made him dizzy. Fred shook him.

"Yeah, I did," Nick replied.

Fred and Olivia cursed and swore.

"No," Nick tried to explain. "He wants me to be his assistant. I can learn whatever magic he's using and turn it against him."

Fred stared at him, dumbfounded. "You have no idea what he's capable of.

"You never have any faith in me," Nick complained. "If this were Alison's idea you wouldn't be shooting it down."

Before Fred or Olivia could respond, they all noticed the sun through the window had faded and the bustle near the wharves had died down. The distant sound of buzzing grew louder and nearer. Nick looked out and saw those strange birds from out in the harbour approaching the house. But as they got nearer, he realized they weren't crows or gulls; they were giant dragonflies. One the size of his forearm hovered in front of the window, considering Nick with its massive, globular eyes before rejoining the swarm. The sound of droning wings became deafening.

Fred sat Nick down on the day bed.

"Look at me!" Fred said, shouting over the racket. "We've got to get you out before he finds out you're here. Close your eyes and think about your apartment. Focus on every detail no matter how small!"

"I..."

"Do it!"

"You have to try and break the contract!" Olivia said to Nick. "Try and cross your name out or destroy the ledger."

Nick nodded. Before he could speak the noise abruptly stopped. He looked out the window and saw the dragonflies forming into a black shape.

"He's coming!" Olivia cried, looking out the window.

"We're out of time!" Fred barked. "Focus on your apartment, the couch, where you were before you came here. Think about every exact detail as hard as you can. Anything tactile that can bring you back to your physical body."

Nick closed his eyes and tried to concentrate. He thought about his couch, the television, and the beer he'd been drinking. Suddenly his hand felt cold. He pictured the rug beneath his feet, and he could feel its ropey texture. The faint sound of voices from the TV crept in. A loud crash disrupted his concentration. Something burst through the door. Nick opened his eyes, but he couldn't discern what he was looking at. He was back in his apartment, but it was like a transparent film over what was happening in this living room. It felt like there was a vac-uum sucking his consciousness out from the back of his head, away from Cachot Cove. The image of his apart-ment grew sharper, while his parents grew weaker, like waking from a dream in slow motion. Just before he was completely gone, he tried to hold on a bit longer, to see what threatened his parents.

"Go!" Fred yelled at Nick.

Nick looked up and saw a tall dark figure towering over his father. It must have stood nine feet tall.

"You can't have him!" Fred yelled, but the figure swat-ted him away easily.

It came towards Nick. He tried to pull himself away. And there it was: Moore's face. Except it was twisted and distorted. Kirk Douglas smiling sickeningly with a shark's grin stretching ear to ear. The details of the apart-ment hardened, and Cachot Cove evaporated. But before Nick could fully extract himself, he felt a huge cold hand on his shoulder, so cold that it burned his skin through his clothes. He opened his eyes and began to scream in pain. Falling to the floor, he rolled around clutching his shoulder.

"Nick!" Charlotte screamed from upstairs, racing down the stairs. "What's wrong?"

She put her hands on him and Nick flailed away from her. He looked around the apartment and realized he was back home. But before he could do anything else, he had to do something about the searing pain in his shoulder. He pulled off his sweater to see. It looked pink and raw like a sunburn and felt like cold plastic when he touched it. He realized the shoulder itself was numb.

"How did you do that?" Charlotte asked. "It looks like frost burn."

"Can't explain," Nick answered. "What do I do?"

Charlotte grabbed Nick's phone and Googled "frost burn." He needed to soak it in warm water. She helped him up to the shower where he stripped down and used the detachable head to run warm water over his shoulder. Slowly, after an intense feeling of pins and needles, it started to feel normal. He turned off the shower and put a cloth over the area.

Together they lay in bed and Nick explained everything as best he could, quickly, without giving the analytical part of his brain a chance to rationalize what had happened at the merchant's mansion. Nick described everything that had happened in a stream-of-consciousness dramatic monologue.

Charlotte just stared, incapable of interrupting.

* * *

Alistair Moore was in control of time.

If the definition of insanity was doing the same thing over and over again and expecting different results, then what did it mean to delight in doing the same thing over and over again and getting the same result? Every day, the sun rose on the nothing-new here in his Cachot Cove, and every day he took pleasure in it. No, he couldn't be insane. Crazy people sat in the corner of a room covered in their own filth, fantasizing about their own imaginary world. Moore wasn't fantasizing: he'd created it. If anything, he suffered from an overabundance of sanity. It was a heavy crown to wear to be a small-time god.

Moore came down for his breakfast. In the dining room, servants scurried about, filling his long table with food. There were eggs, fried and hard boiled, bacon, fried bologna, fish and brewis, fish cakes, fresh fruit, fresh cream, coffee, and strudels—his favourite. The servants waited with heads bowed while he made his choices in case there was something there they hadn't anticipated. He sat and gorged on a bit of everything, starting with some slices of freshly baked bread generously slathered with chunky partridgeberry jam. Tarty juice ran down the corner of his mouth as he re-filled it with bologna and fish cakes heaped with mustard, washing it all down with creamy coffee. His stomach was swollen and uncomfortable.

He'd once estimated he ate about 10,000 calories a day, a diet befitting an Olympic swimmer. But maintaining Shangri-La was hard work and he needed fuel. When he was done eating, he closed his eyes and visualized a bookcase of ledgers. He took down the one labelled "metabolism" and divided the amount he'd just ate in half. His stomach rumbled while his body's temperature rose precipitously. The servants in the room stepped back as Moore radiated heat like a furnace. He opened his eyes and felt his stomach flat once again.

To amend his previous meditation on insanity, Moore would have to say that doing the same thing over and over again and expecting the same result was Sisyphean—and we must imagine Sisyphus happy. And Moore was happy. Each new cycle of sunrise and sunset was a contradiction to his father, who refused to see the world as anything else besides a miserable rock in an indifferent universe, where you must assert your will over those around you and drag a living, kicking and screaming, from everyone else fighting over the same sorry scraps. A handful for someone else meant one less handful for you.

But Moore was a benevolent and generous god. In his world, everyone was free to indulge in his abundance. No more uncertainty as to whether there would be enough fish to pay off the merchant and survive the winter. There was no winter and the waters were always plentiful. Every day, his congregation hauled the fish from the sea, split and salted it, weighed their catch, and the next day it all started over again fresh.

He stepped out onto a balcony of his castle and surveyed his paradise. The sun was high and warm, greeting the fisherman out at sea. The harbour's stages bustled with activity. He burst into a swarm of giant dragonflies and took off to inspect the seas. A hundred and more pairs of eyes transmitted their reports to his central consciousness. It was important that his subjects knew that he was present, that he was there in case they needed him. When he was mortal, it used to grate him that he had such a limited vantage point of his operation in Cachot Cove, only able to look out from his window in the mansion. Now, he was omnipresent, omniscient. No one or no thing escaped his grace.

It had been nearly 100 years since his mind and body had totally left behind that cruel mortal coil. By that time, he'd had everything he needed to survive in his Cachot Cove in this version of infinity. He'd left behind the mirror in his old mansion just as a kind of precaution—no reason to sever his connection completely. There was always the

chance he could find new initiates, although he was prepared for the eventuality of the house falling into atrophy.
And perhaps the rest of that Cachot Cove with it. Even in
the 1940s it was clear to him the time of merchants and
Outport Newfoundland was coming to a close. Men like
his father had fought against modernization and central-
ization, but they would only be denied for so long. Confederation with Canada was the most logical eventuality,
only fools denied it. Moore saw the writing on the wall
and decided to pull up stakes from reality. He liked to
think his father would've begrudgingly admired his cold
calculations.

But he never could have anticipated the possibility
that a new set of tenants would've taken over the mansion with the purpose of establishing a bed and breakfast.
In hindsight, he'd been too hasty gorging on Fred and Olivia. It had been so long since his Cachot Cove had new
residents. However, the son offered an exciting new opportunity. He was smart, directionless and in need of a
father figure. Nick would become his apprentice and once
the renovations were complete, The Merchant's Mansion
B&B could attract new initiates from all over the world.
He was eager to expand, to grow, to share.

CHAPTER SIX

"Wow," Charlotte said after Nick was finished talking.

"Yeah," Nick agreed.

She stood up and paced around the room.

"Well?" Nick asked. "Does that make any sense, or am I losing my goddamn mind?"

"Honestly, maybe both," she replied. "What you described sounds like a level of magic that's way beyond anything I'm familiar with. Projecting your consciousness into your own custom-made astral plane is incredibly powerful stuff. And trapping others in there with you?" She threw her hands up. "The bit about Moore creating his own private woods to possibly commune with fay is interesting. That would explain the hag stone. He must have somehow managed to harness a faerie's powers to fuel his own dark magic. That would explain the alternate reality. He carved out his own space in the fay's world and built a bridge between it and the real Cachot Cove."

Nick thought about all the books Moore had and his unnaturally long life dedicated to studying the occult. Brick by brick he'd built a wealth of esoteric knowledge to pull all of that off. What kind of will would it take to achieve that? And to what purpose? To build his own fantasyland to show up his father? It was sick, sociopathic. Moore had clearly gone insane years ago.

"Are you saying Moore is a fay?" he asked.

"No, I don't know so. There's tons of folklore about fairies drawing humans into fairyland and swapping babies with changelings, but I'm not familiar with someone actually becoming one. When fairies take humans, it's usually as a pet. And that's if you're lucky. They see us as lesser creatures. It would be a very strange scenario for a fay to see a human as an equal such that they would grant him their power."

"Maybe he stole it."

Charlotte reflected on this. "This is all speculation. There's no way we can deduce a solution by ourselves."

"OK, what about me and my parents?" he asked. "What is this doing to our brains? It feels like I'm in a constant haze."

"A part of your consciousness must be trapped there. It's like you're caught in his web and he's sucking you dry."

"Let's pull back on the colourful similes here, please?"

"I'm sorry."

"Is there anything we can do? What about, like, a cleansing ritual or whatever?"

"No, I think we're well beyond that." Charlotte was quiet for awhile. "Honestly, this is all just so far beyond my depth that I don't think I can help."

"We have to try something! I don't think dad has much

longer, and mom is spiralling too." Nick and Charlotte both simultaneously realized the consequences of what was at stake. They looked at each other. "Jesus Christ, I don't want to end up like them."

"OK. Let me think." Charlotte paced around the room quicker. Nick watched the logical gears turning in her head. "If he has a fay's powers, it might be reasonable to say he has a fay's weaknesses as well. We can use that to our advantage. Let's see… I know that fay are sticklers for contracts."

"Like all those signatures in the ledger!" Nick exclaimed.

"Yes, exactly. We might be able to force him into accepting a contract that bans him from the house and releases you and your parents."

"What about everyone else there?" Nick asked.

"I'm afraid there's probably not much we can do for them right now. We have to focus on your parents. Maybe cutting off his connection to the house will weaken him enough that the others can eventually escape." Charlotte resumed her pacing. "A cleansing ritual wouldn't be enough to beat him, but it could draw him out. Then we attack him and force him to sign our contract."

"How do we attack him? What are fay weak against?"

Charlotte considered this. "Iron?"

After some thought, Nick grinned.

* * *

"How does it feel," Nick asked as they wandered around the merchant's mansion, "to be inside a bona fide haunted house?"

"This house isn't haunted," Charlotte answered. "It's possessed."

Nick thought about this and silently agreed.

"C'mon," Charlotte urged. "Let's get to work."

In her hands she carried an abalone shell, a stick of sage, and a feather. Nick opened some windows, and she lit the sage. Using the feather, she wafted it gently around the house. He felt the energy of the house stir; the oppressive vibe softened—he couldn't deny it. They made their way up the stairs, and he couldn't help thinking about Frodo and Sam sneaking around Mordor, hiding from Sauron.

When they got to the top floor, Charlotte lay the shell holding the burning sage on the floor. She examined the tendrils stretching across the room. They were thick and pulsating now. Nick figured the house knew why they were there and wasn't trying to play coy anymore. It was ready for a fight. Charlotte turned her attention to the mirror, coming close but not touching it.

"He must have used this as a conduit, a passageway."

Nick grabbed the ledger. In his pockets were a handful of pens, pencils, and markers. First, he tried a black permanent marker. He drew a fat line across his name, but the ink quickly evaporated. He tried dragging the tips of sharpened pencils across the pages to tear it up, but it was like stone. Finally, he retrieved a lighter and tried setting it on fire. The flames licked the ledger harmlessly. It wasn't even warm. He looked to Charlotte, who shrugged. It wasn't going to be that easy.

Charlotte took out the bag of salt and poured a large ring for the two of them to sit cross legged in the middle of the room with the burning sage between them. She also laid out a number of crystals, which she'd charged on the last full moon.

"This is it," she said. "Last chance to back out."

"Let's do this," Nick said.

"Remember," she reminded him. "He's probably got all kinds of illusion spells. There's no telling what we might see or feel or experience once I start. But as long as we stay in the circle, we should be fine."

"'Should?'" Nick repeated.

Charlotte shrugged. "I told you I'm out of my depth here. Maybe we should…"

"No. We have to try."

"Before we try and cleanse the house, we have to cleanse ourselves," Charlotte explained then saw the hesitant expression on Nick's face. "Otherwise, it's like mopping a floor wearing dirty shoes."

Nick was all in at this point. "Alright," he agreed, "I'll follow your lead."

"Repeat after me: I live in harmony of mind, body, and spirit."

"I live in harmony of mind, body, and spirit."

"I release all energies that do not serve me."

"I release all energies that do not serve me."

"I am filled with love, light, and peace."

"I am filled with love, light, and peace."

"I call all of my power back to me now."

"I call all of my power back to me now."

"I call in protection from negative energy."

"I call in protection from negative energy."

Normally, he'd cringe from this woo woo stuff, but anxiety drove his commitment and intentionally. And once they were finished, he felt like his battery had been recharged. The brain fog he'd been experiencing for the last—what? weeks? months? —was burned off, replaced by a golden light shining within his chest. Even the dull ache in his shoulder had lessened.

"How do you feel?" Charlotte asked.

"Like I just chugged a Red Bull," Nick answered.

"Good. Now the real work begins. Repeat after me: I command any negativity, any low vibrational energy, and nonbenevolent beings within this space to leave and go to the light. You are not welcome here. I command you to leave and go to the light."

Before Nick could repeat what she'd said, the house started to shake. Wood groaned and cracked. He looked to Charlotte. She nodded.

"I command any negativity…"

CRACK

"…any low vibrational energy…"

GROAN

"…and nonbenevolent beings within this space to leave and go to the light…

SMASH

"…you are not welcome here!"

BANG

"I command you to leave and go to the light!"

The shaking turned into violent seizures. Nick opened his eyes and looked around. They were tossing and turning like a ship in a storm.

"No!" Charlotte said. "Sit still. He's trying to knock us out of the circle."

Nick closed his eyes and realized that while the house was shaking around them, the space within the circle was still, unaffected.

"Think about your parents," she continued. "Reach out to them. Ask them for strength."

Nick meditated, focusing on Cachot Cove, where his parents remained trapped. He stretched his mind towards them until he ran up against a wall. *Why bother?* the wall said. *They don't believe in you. They never did. They nurtured you all they could, but you couldn't overcome your nature. It's no use. You're a useless screw-up, a ne'er do well. Second-class to your sister.*

Charlotte could see the struggle in Nick's expression. She could also see the ligament from his neck to his shoulder spasming.

"Don't listen to him!" she yelled. "He's lying!"

But he wasn't lying, was he? Nick knew what the wall was telling him was true. There was no denying it. He was a loser. Try as he may, he'd never measure up. Hockey, music, school, writing—he was always going to be a mediocrity.

"Nick!" Charlotte screamed. "Say it: I release all energies that do not serve me."

"Why?" Nick answered. "It's pointless."

"Just say it. For me."

"I release all energies that do not serve me."

He felt a jolt in his chest, like he'd chugged another Red Bull. The voice in his head faded and the bulkhead banging up against his mind became transparent. On the other side he saw his parents. Fred and Olivia reached out to him, giving him strength.

"You are not welcome here!" Nick yelled at the house. "All the negative bullshit or whatever—just get the fuck out of here!"

The house went still. Nick and Charlotte opened their eyes and looked at each other.

"Nice improvising," she said.

"Is that it?" he asked.

Everything went inky black. Nick thought he'd gone blind and released an unintentional squeal he wasn't proud of. Charlotte began to repeat the mantra and the crystals shone, supplying a dim light.

They spoke together. "I cleanse my home of any heaviness and negativity."

There was a faint noise of clicking. Before Nick could ask what the sound was, he saw that the floor around the circle was crawling with insects. They piled atop each other, trying to break through. The swarm grew until the circle was encased in a crawling cylinder of bugs. They squeaked and squirmed over each other. Nick closed his eyes and re-focused, finding Charlotte's voice among the noise. He resumed the mantra with her. Eventually, he noticed the noise of the insects diminished until there was a loud bang. The wall shook and the mirror fell forward and smashed on the floor, revealing the nexus where all the streaks along the walls converged. They shone with glowing green energy, pulsating towards the nexus where the mirror had been.

BOOM

Something was trying to break through the wall.

Wood and plaster cracked. Nick opened his eyes and saw a form begin to take shape on the far wall. It was a face. The wood and plaster split and cracked to form Moore's hideous grin. The house groaned into a cadence of pops and splinters. Nick realized it was a laugh.

Black ooze poured from Moore's mouth, burning the wood and plaster. Nick could see smoke rising from it, could feel the heat. It smelt like rotten eggs and burning tar. The bugs squealed and tried to flee the ooze. It soon filled the room, sloshing against the walls, but still unable to break the circle's boundary. The light of the crystals contrasted brightly against the liquid's blackness. Nick could see shapes taking form in the ooze. He recognized them as the people he'd seen in Cachot Cove.

"Stop!" they cried. "He's killing us!"

"Nick!" a woman's voice cried. "Husband!"

This broke Charlotte's focus. It was the woman from his vision, the one who said Moore had promised him to her. Charlotte looked to Nick questioningly, but he couldn't find the words to explain.

The people disintegrated within the ooze, like they were being digested. Nick felt like he was going to be sick. That's when he saw his parents. They didn't speak to him, only reached out mournfully. He couldn't bear to watch that. Closing his eyes, he fought to give Charlotte all his energy.

"I command any negativity, any low vibrational energy, and nonbenevolent beings within this space to leave and go to the light. You are not welcome here. I command you to leave and go to the light."

He spoke the mantra until his body was seized with

searing pain, starting from his shoulder and working its way into his chest and mind. He fell to the floor, writhing in pain. Charlotte never stopped her chanting. The writhing got worse until Nick felt disconnected from his body, watching it from above. It turned into a full-on seizure and Nick realized what was happening: Moore had left his mark on his shoulder when he grabbed him and was now using it to take control of his body. Nick could feel the alien presence in his body and focused to resist it, but it was too late. His flailing legs kicked the circle of salt and broke the seal.

He opened his eyes, back in control of his body. The floor beneath him rumbled. He looked to Charlotte, who stared back at him, scared. The floor rumbled again, violently, knocking them out of the circle. Before he could get his bearings, the black ooze swelled like the ocean's waves and picked him up, throwing him down the hall. He swam against the waves, towards Charlotte, but the hallway elongated, the house groaning with the effort. The black waves tossed him over the staircase, the ooze burning his skin. He clutched at the railings to slow his fall, but his hands were slick with viscous oil. He slipped and collided with the bottom floor. Using his vestigial athleticism, he instinctively rolled to distribute some of that impact.

"Nick!" Charlotte cried out. "Help!"

Lying on his back, he looked up to see the staircase spiralling upwards. Charlotte hung trapped in a web. He pushed himself up and his joints collectively screamed. The house groaned as the staircase stretched further upwards, twisting and turning away from him until Charlotte sounded like a whimper. From the shadows appeared Moore with the body of a giant, winged spider, rushing towards him from a thick strand, carrying with him a noxious wind. He landed above Nick with sickening grace. Moore still had that uncanny-valley, movie-star looks with a muscular naked torso attached from his hips to the spider's abdomen, which was armoured with a black carapace. Nick tried to crawl away, but Moore towered over him. Two claws seized Nick and brought him up to Moore's face.

"You're mine now," Moore said. "And I'll take your girlfriend, too. But you won't be working in the harbour, enjoying the sunshine and fresh air with everyone else. I'll build a special dungeon for the two of you where you'll rot for eternity and a day. I'll torture you endlessly until you imagine Dante's *Inferno* as an Eden."

Moore beat his leathery wings and began rising to the top of the staircase. Nick looked up and could see a swirling whirlpool, churning the mansion's ceiling into a starry vortex. Beyond that, Nick could see Cachot Cove, waiting for him like a prison. Moore had him grasped by the shoulders, so he could still manoeuvre his elbows. He reached into his hoodie's pocket and retrieved his nuclear weapon: his father's iron railway spike. He drove it through Moore's abdomen. Moore howled in pain and they fell back down to earth, rushing towards the mansion's bottom floor. Nick hugged Moore's mutant body and used him as a cushion against the crash. They struck the floor and Nick bounced off Moore.

He staggered to his feet and saw Moore writhing on the floor, his size shrinking. The railroad spike had him stuck to the floor, like a pinned butterfly. Nick stood above him and stomped on the spike with his Doc Marten. Moore cried. Nick did it again. Moore's monstrous form receded, dissolving into a shrivelled old man. Now he looked more like Kirk Douglas of 2016 than Spartacus.

"Please," Moore pleaded. "It burns!"

"This house is mine now," Nick said. "I'm severing your connection to it."

"OK!" Moore agreed.

"And let my parents go."

"Anything!"

Nick was emboldened. "And everyone else from Cachot Cove. They're not your prisoners anymore."

"Fine!"

Charlotte joined them. She was holding the ledger.

"Destroy it," Nick said.

Moore nodded. The ledger slowly disintegrated in Charlotte's hands. She let it go, and it scattered into dust.

"Release me!" Moore pleaded.

Nick reached down and pulled out the spike. Moore shot upwards towards the vortex. All the air in the house was sucked out, followed by a loud pop. The ceiling sealed shut like a collapsing flower and the merchant's mansion let out an exhale. Charlotte and Nick lurched into the living and threw themselves onto the couch. They lay down, Nick's arms wrapped around her waist.

His body was tired and battered, but his mind was filled with a blank intensity. There was some residual magic coursing through him. His heartbeat chugged in his ears like a locomotive. Charlotte was trembling in his arms, breathing heavily. He leaned over and bit her ear.

She groaned and pushed her backside into his crotch. With his left hand he clutched her breasts while his right hand slid into her yoga pants and massaged the wet heat between her thighs. She reached back and undid his jeans then pulled down her pants. When he slipped inside her, he throbbed so heavily he almost finished right there and then like a teenager. She hissed through her teeth at first then moaned with pleasure. He gently rocked his hips back and forth until they were both panting. The pace quickened as she pushed back against him. A sweet electricity filled him, and he could feel it filling her, too. They were grunting now, in rhythm with the couch creaking and bouncing on the floor. Nick exploded into Charlotte and he cried out, slipping into a happy oblivion.

Neither of them had the energy to even pull up their pants. Nick reached over and pulled a blanket draped across the chesterfield to cover them. The magic, or whatever it was, had left his body. He knew it had left hers, too. And the house? He was too tired to think about that right now. He wouldn't have been able to lift his eyelids even if there were a fire. Charlotte grasped his arms, and they both fell into a dreamless sleep.

* * *

Nick opened his eyes. The room was dimly lit by faint light leaking through the window, distilled by curtains. He looked outside and saw that it was dawn. He and Charlotte were still in the same position as when they'd first fallen asleep on the couch. Looking at her, he felt a profound sense of guilt. He'd used her. He put her in danger to help him because she loved him, and he knew she wouldn't have said no. He'd been using her this whole time—not just for this encounter with Moore but ever since they'd started dating. He loved her because she loved him. Her love had been a shelter from the storm his life had been the last year or so. Would he still be with her if his dad weren't sick? He wasn't sure. Then again, he wasn't really sure what the better alternative was. He'd always kept parts of himself hidden from everyone around him. What if now that he was pulling the curtain back for someone, he was just scared, and this was another instance of running when something got too difficult? His head hurt. Now wasn't the time to get into the weeds of all that bullshit. What he really needed was a therapist. A mental plumber to unclog his brain. And a massage therapist judging by how his back felt right now.

Before he moved, he took a deep breath and looked around the living room. The house felt different, less oppressive. He gently shook her awake. They sat up on the couch and Nick instantly felt pain all over his body. He did up his pants and went to the fridge and found some frozen peas in the freezer, which would go very nicely on his swollen knee.

"Did it work?" Charlotte asked.

"I don't know."

He noticed then that all the lights were out. They checked their phones, which were both dead. After letting the frozen peas sit on his knee for about ten minutes, he got up and opened some windows. He found the circuit panel and reset the breakers. The merchant's mansion lit up and they both looked around in amazement. For perhaps the first time, he recognized that it really was a beautiful house.

"I think we did it," she said in a near whisper.

Outside, they could hear birds chirping nearby. They both looked at each other with excitement. It was a revitalizing sound. Nick went outside to the car and fetched his bag of sunflower seeds then tossed a handful on the grass. A few nervous chickadees darted over and seized some. Nick took the rest of the sunflower seeds and scattered them across the property, never so happy in his life to see crows and squirrels. Even a blue jay made an appearance, bullying the smaller birds.

"Nick!" Charlotte called out from the door.

He looked and saw the nervousness in her face then ran back inside.

"What's wrong?" he asked.

"I plugged in our phones and there's bunch of missed calls from your sister. On both our phones."

His stomach sank. He called Alison without bothering to go through the backlog of voicemails and texts.

"Where the hell have you been?" she demanded.

"Sorry, our phones got wet and we were drying them out." It was the best he could come up with at the moment.

"Dad took a turn for the worse. He's in palliative care."

Nick's head spun.

"You need to get over there as fast as you can," Alison's voice broke. "They don't think he has very long."

"What about you?"

"I'm at Pearson right now trying to get a flight. I might be able to get in late tonight if I'm lucky."

"OK, good luck."

Alison hung up. Nick stood in the living room, unable to speak.

"Is it your dad?" Charlotte asked eventually.

Nick nodded.

"Is he dying?" she asked after a pause.

Nick nodded.

She put a hand on his shoulder and guided him over to the couch. They sat down and both stared at the floor in silence. His mind vacillated between images of his father in Cachot Cove and in the hospital bed. Gradually, the former faded while the latter sharpened. A deep feeling of dread formed as his mind articulated the obvious question. Not wanting to think about that, he stood up.

"We have to get going," he said and hurried out of the house towards the car.

Charlotte scrambled to catch up. She barely had the passenger door closed when Nick pulled into gear and started driving. The kilometres rolled by in silence as they approached Carbonear.

"Nick?" Charlotte asked. He knew what she was going to say. It was the same question he'd been dreading. "Did we do this?"

* * *

His father's breaths came in short staccatos. A tube connected from a machine and wrapped around his head helped Fred breathe. The time between each breath felt like an eternity. His lids opened listlessly to reveal lifeless eyes staring up at the ceiling. Nick gently smoothed them shut with his palm, but they kept stubbornly popping back open. The nurses were "snowing" him, giving him medication to reduce his pain and suppress his respiration and thus hasten his death. It sounded like a fair deal to Nick. He took a swab and dipped it in a cup of water to rub his father's lips, the only way he could take hydration.

Charlotte sat beside him. She looked to Nick with pleading eyes. He knew what she wasn't saying: *Did we do this?* The same question she'd asked in the car on the drive over. He didn't have an answer then and he didn't have one now.

Fred was in a private palliative care room. Beside the bedroom where his father was dying was a guest room with two large couches and a closet. Nick imagined he'd be spending a night or two on one of those couches, further constricting his spine, which was starting to feel like a compressed coil, although he wondered how long anyone could live like this. But deep down he knew that his father would fight for life, however unconsciously, until Alison arrived. He looked over at Charlotte and saw the exhaustion in her face.

"We've had an insane day or two," Nick said. "Have a nap on the couch. I'll stay up with dad."

"Are you sure?"

"Yeah, I'd like some time alone with him, to be honest."

She paused like she was going to put up a fight, but Nick could tell she was relieved. After giving him a kiss, she went out on the couch. He heard some rustling on the couch as she got comfortable then, after just a few minutes, gentle snoring. They must have slept about twelve hours following the encounter with Moore, but Nick still felt exhausted.

As he sat with father while he took his final sips of life, Nick was baffled at how this man, who used to feel so larger than life, who once contained an ocean of frustration, love, fear, hope, and anxiety, was reduced to this husk. Moore had extracted everything from him. Had Nick been too late? Had Fred been beyond any hope of recovery? Or had he made things even worse? He needed answers. He had to try. He closed the curtains and shut the door. The only light in the room came from the blinking light of the breathing machine. Nick concentrated on the dark contours of his father's face and focused on his breath, getting in sync with his dad's rhythm but with deeper inhalations and longer exhalations. Eventually they were on the same wavelength. Nick closed his eyes and thought about Cachot Cove, where Moore held his parents prisoner.

"You did well," Fred whispered hoarsely. "Moore won't be able to get you anymore. Or anyone else."

Nick's face buckled hearing his father—his real, physical father—speak for the first time in over a year.

"I thought I could save you," he said. "I'm afraid I made things worse."

Fred shook his head. "This isn't your fault. You did good. It was too late for me."

"What about mom?"

"Nick?" a new voice asked. "What's going on?"

The room was suddenly illuminated with harsh light. Nick squinted and looked around to find Alison. What time was it? He checked his watch. 8:33 pm. That short parley had taken the entire afternoon.

"I was just talking to dad," he managed.

Alison was about to speak when they both turned to their father. His breathing had changed. It was rapid and shallow.

"Oh Jesus," Alison said and ran out to the hallway looking for a nurse. "Help!"

Nick held a hand to his father's chest. He could feel his heart beating frantically, thudding against his rib cage. Alison returned with a nurse.

"I think this is it," the nurse said to Alison. "He was holding on for you, honey."

In a matter of seconds, the intensity of Fred's heart dropped. Now, instead of Jon Bonham's bass drum, it felt like a little weak bird fluttering inside a cage. And then nothing. Fred let out a long gasp then lay still, not moving after several seconds. The machine continued to pump air into Fred's nose, but he wasn't breathing. The nurse came around and removed it. Alison began to cry and hugged the nurse. Nick slumped into his chair and stared at his father's body. Fred hadn't answered his question, but Nick knew when his dad was bullshitting him. He had to try and contact him again.

Alison bent over their dad and whispered something in his ear Nick couldn't hear.

"I'm going to see mom," she said eventually.

"Are you going to tell her what happened?" Nick asked.

"I don't know. I just feel like I need to see her."

She took one last brief look at their dad then left the room with fresh tears. Nick came out and found Charlotte sitting on the couch, her red eyes still holding the same question: *Did we do this?* Nick sat down and held her hand.

"One more try," he said.

He went back into the room. As he turned to close the door, his shoulder burned. When he turned to face his father, he saw him laughing hideously. It was Moore. He turned away, unable to look.

"You were both very clever," Moore said. "The iron spike was an especially nice touch. Well done."

"I banished you," Nick said, his eyes closed. "You're violating our agreement."

"That's right," Moore replied. "You did. You banished me from the house. But I still have some connection to you." Nick unconsciously rubbed his shoulder. "But it won't last much longer. No matter. I know when I've been beaten."

"And what about my parents? And everyone else you trapped?"

Moore laughed again. "Yes, unfortunately that was the only flaw in your plan. Otherwise, I must say, it was expertly executed. I can't say that enough, although I think most of the credit is owed to your whore."

"What are you talking about?"

"You should've listened to your mother and gone to law school, then you would've known about contract negotiations and loopholes. I, on the other hand, am very familiar with contracts. You should've specified I had to release your parents before severing my connection to the house. You see, even though they're free, they have no way back to their bodies. They can only peek through, like the bars of a prison cell."

"What about me? I'm free."

"Yes, you only had a brief attachment. You will recover fine, no worse than a few days of heavy drinking, which I understand you're quite familiar with. But the others, their consciousnesses are here lock, stock, and barrel. Their downloads are complete—if I were to use your modern language. I will miss the old stomping grounds, and it was nice to taste some fresh meat after so long, but I have everything I need now. Good luck selling the house. Maybe that bitch of yours can find a nice mantra to facilitate the sale."

Fred's face split into a horrific grimace of laughter. The sound rose into a terrifying crescendo. Nick slapped his palms over his ears. Just as he thought his eardrums and mind were about to pop, everything went silent. After some hesitation, he lifted his hands. Moore was gone. Fred's body lay in the bed. Nick approached his father and lay a hand on Fred's face. He felt like a failure of a son, but he'd grown used to that, hadn't he?

Opening the door, he found Charlotte waiting eagerly. He nodded.

"It worked," he lied. "They're fine now."

Charlotte watched him dubiously but said nothing. She followed him to the elevator then out of the hospital.

CHAPTER SEVEN

"I'm sorry to have to tell you this," the doctor explained. "But I don't think it's a good idea for your mother to attend your father's funeral."

Nick and Alison sat in the doctor's office unable to find words. Nick liked his mother's doctor. He was kind, didn't rush, and didn't throw a bunch of jargon at them. Whenever they sat down with him, it felt like they had all of his attention. If he had to guess, Nick would say he was Nigerian. He couldn't pronounce "Nwachukwu," so he just referred to him as "Doctor." He wondered how many locals bemoaned they had a Come From Away for a doctor. Newfoundlanders had a habit of alienating outsiders, not to mention any racism foreign healthcare workers probably dealt with here on the job. If anything, Nick was happy this guy wasn't part of the old boys' club and their spoiled brats that made up most of the doctors in the province.

"Despite the encouraging initial recovery from the stroke, she seems to be slowly deteriorating," the doctor continued. "It's hard to tell how she's interpreting what's going on around her, but I'm afraid that an emotional experience like her husband's funeral would set her back beyond a point of no return."

A part of Nick was relieved that they wouldn't have to deal with the logistics of getting their mother to St. John's. They would've had to get her into a wheelchair and arrange for a cab or bus to take her there and back. He also didn't want to think about the reactions of the people attending, those pitying glances. People didn't have any tact at funerals; they wanted all the morbid details. They saw you lying there with your guts hanging out and wanted to extract every last inch of entrail.

Alison suddenly stood up and walked out of the office. Nick watched her go and wasn't sure what to say. The doctor, likely used to all kinds of reactions to bad news, didn't react.

"Uhh...thanks for everything," Nick managed then chased after Alison down the hall.

"I'm getting a lawyer," she said. "He can't keep mom here for the funeral. She needs to go."

"What if he's right?"

"What?"

"What if it did set mom back like he said?"

Alison shook her head and set her chin in that stubborn defiance he knew so well. But she was out of her depth here, and they both knew it.

"Mom would want to be there," she said. "It's not fair."

"Of course, but we can't take that chance."

"I have to get out of here." She turned and walked towards the door.

Nick wasn't going to argue. They got in his car and

drove towards St. John's. Alison turned on the radio and "Grey Foggy Day" started to play, and she immediately switched it to another channel. She stared out the window, sniffling and wiping away whatever tears dared drip from her eyes. Nick sought the words that would bridge this gap, but they remained buried under a mound of dumb silence. He'd imagined this shared pain would bind them together, but, as usual, they remained alone together. It was like a bandit had come into the room and shot them each in the chest; while they shared the same pain, it was pain they could only experience individually.

As the kilometres rolled by, Nick thought about the eulogy for his dad he was composing in his mind. It was a morbid thing to admit, but he'd actually been looking forward to it. After all, he was a writer, and writing was how he processed his thoughts and emotions. Was it really so ghoulish to crave that catharsis? To arrange his feelings and deliver them to friends and family. Wasn't that the whole point of a eulogy? This was finally his chance to get out of his head and write from the heart. Why not lean into it? He'd been through so much bullshit this past year or more, it was time to transform that pain into something productive. Delivering his father's eulogy would be his way to rise from the ashes and begin this new chapter in his life fresh.

"I was talking to Uncle Jim," Alison said after a long silence. "He wants to do dad's eulogy."

"OK," Nick replied.

* * *

When Nick got home, he went through the text messages and DMs he'd received from friends and family about his dad. His eyes glazed over words like "condolences," "sorry," and "loss," until one text caught his attention: *sorry about your dad bro gimme a shout if you need anything.* It was from his old buddy Phil who played bass in one of his bands back in the day. He was still listed as "Landphil" in his phone, the nickname he'd been assigned in high school. They hadn't spoken in a couple years, not since Nick started taking school seriously. He felt compelled to text back.

Thanks, Nick replied.

How ya been? Phil texted back within minutes.

Not gonna lie, been tough with dad being sick and I lost my job at uni

Going at tonight?

No plans

Wanna get on the go?

Yeah sure

Come over to my place, I'm just playing Xbox

Nick realized then that this was exactly the outcome he was hoping for when he first responded. Phil was always that guy who was holding something or could easily get his hands on it: weed, shrooms, coke, just about anything. And Nick was feeling that old itch to spend all day playing video games, getting high, and listening to punk rock.

Phil hadn't specified where "my place" was exactly, so Nick assumed he was still living in his parents' basement apartment. On the way over, he stopped by a Marie's to grab some cans of India and a few bags of Doritos. Fuck it, might as well get a pack of Export As while he was at it, too. As he parked on the sidewalk outside Phil's house, he saw that he'd had the misfortunate timing of catching Phil's parents as they were leaving the house. Here we go, Nick thought.

"Hi, Nick," Phil's mom said. "So sorry to hear about your dad. And your poor mother."

"At least he's no longer in pain," Phil's dad observed.

"Yes," Nick agreed, "that's true."

He held the bag of goodies with one hand and gave them both an awkward one-armed hug. They eyed him with that pitying curiosity. He hated himself for feeling resentful; they were good people. What he really resented was the human thirst for tragedy. To gobble it up like a pack of hyenas whenever a corpse presented itself on the veldt. And those pat responses: *sorry for your loss, he's no longer in pain, let me know if you need anything*. They all went through Nick like nails on a chalkboard.

"Well, Phil will be happy to see you," his mom said after they were standing awkwardly in the driveway for what felt like a lifetime.

Nick smiled and made for the basement. He was about to knock when he remembered Phil hated having to get up off the couch to let people in. Stepping through the doorway, it felt like going back in time. Everything was the same as the last time he'd been here, which was probably five or six years ago. He still had the same *Star Wars*, Bad Religion, and *Pulp Fiction* posters up. The place still stunk like weed. Nick still couldn't believe his parents didn't lose their minds over him not even bothering to open a window while he smoked. The only thing that was different was that the 360 had been replaced by an

Xbox One.

"What's up, man," Phil asked, not getting up from the couch.

"This is it," Nick replied.

He joined Phil on the couch and opened a can of India. And while the setting had changed in the half-dozen years since he'd last visited, something else certainly had: Phil was hollow. Not just skinny. He'd always been skinny. Now he seemed like the air might just about blow through him. He didn't look like a junkie or anything, just…lesser. Nick was starting to have second thoughts about this whole thing until Phil played some Municipal Waste and passed him a bong. After a couple pulls, Nick was transported back to a time he didn't have to worry about his parents' health, a career, a mortgage, or a goddamn sorcerer trying to steal his mind.

Phil was a solid bass player and had been in most of the bands Nick had tried to get off the ground ever since high school. He could write songs and was a decent singer, too. The only problem was he was impossible to get motivated. Truth be told, in Nick's experience, most musicians were like herding cats. If everyone agreed to a 6 pm jam time, guaranteed they wouldn't get started until 8:30 pm. It baffled him that talented people doing something fun couldn't all get on the same page and work towards something great. He smiled to himself at that thought. It was probably the exact same way his dad had felt about him when it came to hockey. At least as a writer, he only had himself to blame for not getting his shit together.

They played *Gears of War* and caught up on each other's lives. It didn't take long for them to empty all the cans

Nick had brought. Phil still worked at HMV, but there were rumblings in stores across Canada they were closing soon. The conversation finally turned to Nick's parents.

"Sorry about your folks, man," Phil said. "They seemed pretty intense, but it was cool they let us jam in your basement."

Fred and Olivia used to go to the movies while Nick, Phil, and whatever group of guys they'd managed to scrounge together would try and get through some Bad Religion and Pennywise tracks. Before and after practice, they'd congregate by the basement door under the back patio and smoke joints, dropping their roaches in an empty margarine tub Nick would hide under some rocks. Eventually, Fred had discovered the receptacle and brought it to Nick. "I found your secret stash," Fred said. Nick wasn't sure how to reply. "At least you're not smoking it in the house," Fred added. And that was that. Now that he thought about it, it hadn't occurred to Nick that most of his other buddies' parents never let them jam in their houses.

"De-Mons are playing at Distortion tonight," Phil mentioned. "First show they've played in a couple years. Want to go?"

Nick hadn't planned on going downtown but he had a good buzz now and felt like chasing it. "Yeah, sounds good."

"How about some zombie lines?" Phil asked.

Nick nodded and they grinned at each other. Phil called a cab while he retrieved three separate bags of cocaine, ketamine, and MDMA and mixed them together. He chopped up two thick, brownish white lines and handed Nick a rolled up twenty-dollar bill. The astringent mix of powdered chemicals burned his nostril. It only took about five minutes before he felt his body warming up. The mopey tiredness he'd been feeling the last forty-eight hours was replaced by a chatty, cocaine-fuelled confidence.

The cab pulled up outside. On the way out, Nick put his arm around Phil. "I can't wait to get in the fucking pit with you, brother."

They chittered like chimpanzees in the cab ride downtown. George Street, which Nick had always dismissed as a tacky, touristy meat market, beckoned him. Young girls wore spaghetti string tops and short skirts, despite the early spring nip. Agro bros in their nicest, night-out American Eagle buttoned shirts eyed him with hostility, but Nick didn't even notice them. Phil started walking towards Distortion, and Nick reluctantly followed. Up on the deck, which connected Distortion, The Levee, CBTGs (Closest Bar to Gulliver's), and the Bull and Barrel, a crowd was smoking and chatting. A few locked eyes with Nick, flashing recognition, but he didn't want to get pulled into a conversation, so he hustled up the stairs to Distortion.

He ordered a beer and listened to the opening band. Behind the bar was an aquarium with a couple fish floating around. He stared at them, drinking his India, envying their simple little lives. The cocaine had worn off, but the ketamine kicked in just in time. The floor felt like a waterbed as he walked around the bar in a disassociated, dream-like state. A numbness filled his body, and the myriad anxieties that once filled his mind floated away like helium balloons. He looked up and laughed as he watched them drift away. His brain felt like a pot of Kraft Dinner being stirred gently by a small wooden spoon. Phil put his arm around him, and they made silly, contorted faces at each other, laughing like maniacs. When Nick tried to lift his arms, his left felt as heavy as a sandbag, but his right shot up like a wacky inflatable tube man. And as ridiculous as he was sure he looked, he didn't give a shit. He felt happy to be alive for the longest time he could remember.

Then the unreality started to feel a little too real, like he was back at the merchant's mansion, battling with Alistair Moore over his mind. The world slipped away, and the once pleasant complacency of that earlier disassociation became filled with anxiety. His heart pumped hard in his chest, and he could feel it whooshing in his ears, drowning out the music. He realized he was falling into a k-hole. But just before he was about to be overcome with delirium, the MDMA swooped in and rescued him. Now, instead of feeling like a free-range radical bouncing around in isolation, he felt a wave of euphoria rush him into the collective energy of the bar. He was connected to the floor, the walls, the music, and everything around him. A mouthful of India was the most delicious beer he'd ever tasted, and he needed to drink every millilitre of it in the bar.

De-Mons took the stage, and he absolutely needed to get in the pit, to feel his body colliding against others like he was inside a particle accelerator. He crashed and banged with the furious energy of skate punk and breakdowns, not feeling the impact of elbows and shoulders against his clenched jaw. Despite not knowing any of the lyrics, he raised his fist and shouted nonsense along with everyone else. Beer splashed over the crowd upon impact between bodies, and Nick watched in awe as the liquid arced with the curving trajectory of gravity's rainbow. Between songs, he was able to catch his breath while the skinny guitar player ran through the next song's riffs, doing his own little practice session alone on stage. The band watched with awkward impatience as he jogged his memory. Then the drummer, slick with sweat, counted them in. To mosh was a joyful fury. Pushing and bumping into other humans was an explosion of Dionysian vigor. De-Mons finished their set with a cover of "Infested" by Choking Victim, and Nick made sure to exhaust whatever energy he had left in the tank.

The bar cleared and everyone went out on the deck to smoke. The frigid air chilled Nick's sweaty shirt, but it felt more comforting than cold. He felt pleasantly exhausted as he passed a joint around with Phil, the members of De-Mons, and Distortion's owner. They went back inside, and it passed last call, so the owner locked the door, and they continued drinking in the empty bar. Nick drank quietly, staring at the fish floating inside the aquarium, deep inside his own MDMA buzz.

"Hey!" the bar owner said a couple times before Nick realized he was talking to him. Everyone laughed but he just kept grinning like Forrest Gump. "I'll give you a triple rum and Coke if you eat one," he said, pointing at the aquarium.

Without hesitation, Nick approached the fish tank and dunked his arm in, managing to grab a fat tetra. He dropped it in his mouth and swallowed without chewing. The little fish swam straight down his esophagus. The guys from De-Mons were falling over each other laughing.

"That's fucked up, man," the owner said shaking his head and slid Nick his drink as promised.

He gulped down his triple of Screech and Coke to wash out the flavour of fish tank and propel the tetra down into his gut. The MDMA was wearing off now and his head started to feel greasy. The drummer from De-Mons chopped up a few lines on the bar for everyone, which gave Nick the boost he needed to go fetch a cab home. His jaw was wired so tight now he could barely speak. He tapped Phil on the shoulder and waved goodbye then stumbled out onto George Street.

He got into the nearest cab and managed to grunt his address to the driver. There was an ambulance parked on the corner of George and Adelaide, its siren silently oscillating. A couple paramedics and police were standing around a guy lying on the cobblestone street in a puddle of his own puke. Nick felt the tetra inside his stomach backflip, and he had to look away before he painted the street with his vomit. The streetlights glared angrily at him, and he had to keep his eyes on his feet during the ride. But when he looked away, the image of his parents trapped in Cachot Cove with Moore filled his thoughts, so he forced himself to look at the blurry townhouses sliding by the window, making him nauseous. When the cabbie stopped in front of his address, he retrieved a twenty from his wallet and shoved it in the guy's hand.

After a few failed attempts, he got his key into the lock and opened his apartment door. The hallway was dark. He groped for the light switch while trying to pull his sneakers off at the same time. Lacking the coordination to pull this off, he tumbled and crashed through the closet doors. He lay in the pile of coats and splintered wood. The lights switched on and Charlotte was standing above him.

"Jesus, Nick," she said, "you're a state. Where the hell were you? You didn't answer any of my texts or calls."

"It didn't work!" Nick croaked.

"What didn't work?" she asked. "What are you talking about?"

"The cleanse or séance or whatever you called it. It didn't work."

Charlotte helped him up to his feet.

"It didn't work," he repeated. "We kicked Moore out, but my parents are still trapped in la-la land with him."

Charlotte stood there, unsure of what to say.

"I'm sorry," she said eventually. "I did my best."

"You said it would work! I should never have listened to you and your bullshit."

"Don't you dare put this on me. I told you we were out of my depth, but you insisted. I warned you."

"You didn't like my parents."

"That's not true. And what are you suggesting? That I did this on purpose?"

"What the hell am I going to do?"

"I'm sorry you're going through all this. But that doesn't excuse you from acting this way."

"You don't get it. No one does."

"You've been through a lot. I'm sure all the stuff about being adopted is tough, too, but you can't just keep blaming other people for your problems. Me, your parents, your sister."

"What are you talking about?"

"You just expect someone to come along and fix all your problems. I know you resent me for my job and not having the same family life as you, but none of that is my fault. It's not your fault either, but it is your responsibility to deal with it. I know that sucks, but it's the truth."

Nick laughed. "That's pretty fucking easy for you to say, isn't it?"

"I've tried to help you, but if you're going to act like this then I'm not going to put up with it."

Nick looked up at her and saw that look of pity he despised. "Oh for fuck sakes, don't look at me like that. Don't give me that phoney sympathetic bullshit look."

Charlotte paused like she was about to say something then walked away. She put on her boots and jacket and started towards the door.

"Where are you going? Your parents'?" Nick stressed *paaaarents* for dramatic emphasis.

Charlotte turned around and regarded him with equal parts sympathy and contempt in the doorway. After a moment of hesitation, the latter won out, and she left. Nick collapsed on the couch, his body shuddering as the MDMA wore off, simultaneously too hot and too cold. His throat was dry and scratchy. He went to the fridge, looking for beer, but there was only coffee creamer. After chugging all of that, he filled up a glass of water and chugged that as well. His stomach churned angrily and he projectile vomited into the sink. The dead tetra lay stuck in the drain, covered in beer and bile. When Nick saw that he began laughing, hot drool dripping from his chin. The laughter eventually transformed into racking sobs as he collapsed onto the kitchen floor. He was alone now, truly alone. His dad was dead, his mom may as well be, his sister had no clue what was going on, and now Charlotte was gone, too. The misery felt like a cold, wet blanket, too heavy to throw off. He lay there, luxuriating in its cold comfort. After he cried himself dry, he fell into a restless sleep, holding himself like a fetus with his back against the fridge.

* * *

KNOCK

Nick stirred on the kitchen floor. His mouth tasted like sawdust and his brain felt like it was filled with it too.

KNOCKKNOCK

The door. Someone was at his door. He pulled himself up and staggered towards the source of the commotion. Looking through the peephole, he saw his sister with a very crooked look on her face.

"Where the hell have you been?" she asked when he let her in. "I've been calling…" she trailed off when she saw the wrecked closet door. "What the hell…" she looked in the kitchen and covered her mouth against the stink. Darting into the living room, she opened a window and stuck her face by the screen for fresh air. "I've been trying to call you," she finally managed to say.

Nick retrieved his cellphone from his pocket and saw that it was dead.

"The funeral starts in one hour," Alison said, her tone flat.

Nick cursed at himself for being so stupid. "I'll get a

quick shower and I'll be ready."

The cold water shocked his system into semi-wakeful-
ness. Two mouthfuls of Listerine followed by a thorough
brushing cleansed his mouth of whatever remnants of
vomit, and tetra, remained. His face was patchy with sev-
eral-days worth of fur, but he didn't have time to shave. In
his closet, he dug up a pair of black slacks and a buttoned
shirt he probably hadn't worn in over a year, which he
managed to squeeze himself into. When he came downstairs, Alison was gone, but the kitchen was clean. There
was a bottle of extra strength Aspirin on the counter; he
took two with a glass of water. She was waiting for him
outside.

"Let's stop by Tim's," she said as they got into the car.
"Get yourself a coffee and a donut or something."

Nick got an XL with three milk and three sugar with
some ice cubes in it, so he could chug it like a milkshake.
The honey cruller helped settle his stomach a little. Once
they pulled up to the Corpus Christi parking lot, Alison
handed him some face cream. "You look like a corpse,"
she said. He couldn't argue.

"Thanks," he said, looking at her. It wasn't just a thanks
for the cream, it was for not lecturing him, for cleaning
up the kitchen, and more importantly, not asking about
Charlotte. Alison knew better than anyone there was no
messing around before game time.

"Are you ready?" she asked.

Nick swallowed the last of his coffee, nodded, then got
out of the car.

Inside the church, he was grateful people simply
gave a curt nod and proceeded to a pew. He felt his shirt

straining to contain his bulging beer belly. Sweat trickled down his neck between his tight collar. He was kind of surprised he didn't burst into flame upon stepping inside. Once the ceremony started, he followed Alison, who carried the urn holding their father's ashes. They took the seats towards the front aisle near the altar. Nick dug his fingernails into his thighs to keep himself from dozing off during the priest's nonsense.

Then it was time for Uncle Jim's eulogy. Nick braced himself for an appalling mishmash of bumbling cliches and saccharine schmaltz, coalescing into a trite bathos. He leaned into his pettiness to relieve his own feelings of shame for not having insisted on doing the eulogy himself. When Alison had brought it up, Nick felt like he couldn't deny Uncle Jim the opportunity to eulogize his brother. But who was he to be so demonstrative? He wasn't around to help their mother when she needed it. In that moment, Nick resented his uncle with burning acrimony.

"When our father died when we were young, I soon learned that grief is like that old drunk that comes knocking when you least expect it and you can never seem to be able to get rid of it when it does," Uncle Jim began, seizing Nick's attention. "What took me longer to learn is that you can't rush it out the door. You have to sit with it, hear it out, listen to what it has to say. And, what I learned later again, is that you shouldn't share a drink with it." Uncle Jim smiled to allow for a few laughs, easing some of the tension. "I think this is something my brother understood long before me. He was a runner as most of you know. A great runner. A great athlete all around. Hockey and baseball too. I used to think he was running from his pain, his grief. Now I know he was running with it. Letting it run its course. One day I asked him why he bothered putting his body through so many miles. The only thing that ended up stopping him was his hip replacement. He told me that he felt closest to dad when he was out running. That after about twenty or thirty minutes, after he got through "the suck" as he called it, the aches and pains would die away, and so would whatever worries he was carrying, and he could feel our dad's presence with him."

Nick had never considered that. To him, it was always about athletics and overcoming challenges; he'd never considered that it was therapeutic.

"Fred turned our father's death into a source of strength, and I always envied that about him. I tried to do the same when he was in hospital during the last stages of his battle with dementia, but it's hard to grieve for someone with Alzheimer's, and I'm not as strong as my big brother. Dementia is death by a thousand paper cuts, a thousand little indignities stacked on top of each other. The person we loved is gone, but he still goes on living. To see my brother, whose life was so defined by activity, lie there and waste away is a cruelty beyond words."

That one hit hard. Beside him, Nick could feel Alison sobbing quietly. He glanced around and saw nearly everyone else in the church sniffling, holding tissues to their eyes. It was a moving eulogy, to be sure, and yet he himself didn't feel the same catharsis as everyone around him. Because he knew that his father wasn't truly dead. Not yet. His body may have been incinerated into ashes, but his mind, his soul, his psyche, whatever the hell you called it, was trapped in Cachot Cove with Moore.

"Death is the only key that can open the door of Alzheimer's," Uncle Jim continued. "And in death, we are able to remember our loved ones in their best selves. Fred wouldn't want us to dwell on how his life ended. He'd want us to feel inspired by his life, and, more importantly, to use it as a source of strength. Like he has been for me through my life."

Nick was disarmed by his uncle's unaffected honesty. He spoke in a language that was clean and pure, trimmed of fat. Very rarely did Nick achieve prose that was so close to the bone. He realized that Uncle Jim had likely burned away any pretensions in the crucible of Alcoholics Anonymous meetings. Nick imagined getting up in front of people battling addictions and what it meant to truly share your experiences in a moment of naked candor. It wouldn't take long before artifices were soon stripped away, exposing the core, what really mattered. And that was what writing was really all about wasn't it? To remove masks you didn't know you wore.

Uncle Jim stepped down and the priest said some more stuff that went in one of Nick's ears and out the other. The procession left the church, and Nick and Alison assumed the duty of standing at the exit to address those leaving. Nick found himself parroting cliches, which he should have despised but it seemed to comfort both the mourners and, honestly, him, too. Something about these familiarities made everyone at ease. People needed predictable inputs and outcomes in these situations. It was simply what one said and did.

Once everyone was gone, Alison turned to Nick. "Aunt Azalea is having people over, are you coming?"

"I don't know," he said. The cocktail of caffeine, Ibu-profen, and honey cruller was starting to wear off and he could really feel his brain starting to turn to jelly.

"You should go."

Nick looked at her and he knew what she really meant: *I don't want to go by myself.* He just wished she'd come out and say it, be real with him for once. But after coming to rescue him this morning, he couldn't deny her this.

"Alright," he said.

* * *

Aunt Azalea lived in King Williams' Estates. Friends and family had gathered within the McMansion, but everyone seemed afraid to sit down lest they knock over some tacky, overpriced knickknack. Aunt Azalea had married some real estate agent whom Nick had probably met half a dozen times his entire life. The guy seemed to travel a lot for work. Nick assumed he was either having multiple affairs or was selling coke. He then lamented this uncle wasn't present at the moment because he could really do with a line. After his dad's funeral, he'd been dying for a joint to take the edge off, but he had to be on his best behaviour. As they walked in through the door, Alison went straight for the booze. At this point, the scent of alcohol made him want to urge.

"How are you, Nick?" It was Mr. Peddle, his old high school French teacher. He'd taught with Nick's parents at some point down the line.

"I'm well, thanks," Nick said then hastily added: "all things considered." Since his father wasn't truly dead, per se, this whole supposed grieving experience felt surreal, but he couldn't let these folk think he was either nuts or callous. Well, he was sure most of them took one look at him and thought he was nuts, but he didn't want to seem indifferent to his father's "death." Maybe they'd just pass it off as, *oh, he's still processing it*. Yeah, that'll work.

As Nick was thinking about all this, he noticed Mr. Peddle was staring at the bottom right part of his jaw. It felt a little tender now that he noticed it. There was probably a greenish bruise hiding beneath the stumble on his grey skin. Collateral damage from last night.

"I read that piece you published in the *Globe and Mail* a few years ago about Putin. I don't know much about Russian history, but I found it fascinating."

"Thanks, I appreciate that."

"Your mother sent it to me, actually. She'd emailed it to a few of us."

There it was again. Just like his dad with hockey. Nick remembered telling his mom that his op-ed had been accepted by the *Globe* and she looked like she was going to puke. "You can always ask them not to publish it," she'd said. That had driven Nick up the wall. It would've been so much simpler if his mom was like Livia Soprano, a hateful, vindictive snake, but it wasn't that simple. What she feared was attention and the possibility of scrutiny and criticism. Like she was afraid he couldn't stand on his own two feet in the world. Of course, when it was out in print, she praised him, but it felt hollow at that point. He supposed he'd internalized that insecurity. It's what kept him from stripping away those masks in his writing and laying it all out there, like his Uncle Jim had during the eulogy. It also kept him from opening up to Charlotte.

For the next couple hours, as he sipped plastic cups of Pepsi, friends and extended family members of his parents told him about how Fred and Olivia liked to brag about him and the exciting stuff he was doing at university, his job at the Writing Centre, and the stuff he was publishing. At first, he lamented that his parents hadn't shared this enthusiasm with him before they became trapped in a madman's metaphysical, psychological prison. But then a thought dawned on him, perhaps they had—he'd just never noticed. He was always so focused on the criticism and nagging that he discounted the praise and encouragement.

Before he could fully come to grips with this realization, he heard something shatter. Everyone turned to look at the source of the noise and saw that Alison had dropped her glass of wine. She held a hand to her forehead, baffled by what happened. Looking around, embarrassed by the attention she'd brought to herself, she took off to the bathroom. Nick was also baffled that it was Alison and not him who'd drank too much and caused a scene. He'd always wanted to see a chink in the armour, a little glimpse of humanity behind his sister's façade, but this was actually uncomfortable to watch. He cleaned up the mess then went and found her in the guest bathroom upstairs.

He knocked on the door. "Alison?"

"I'm OK," she said amid sniffles. "Just give me a minute."

A voice appeared from behind Nick and frightened him. "I think you should take her to her hotel." It was Aunt Azalea. She had a snooty look on her face that seemed to suggest this was somehow his fault. He was about to placate her when he remembered all the times his mother had felt stressed out and nearly brought to tears (she never actually cried) by Aunt Azalea's snobby bullshit. Nothing was ever good enough for her. Now he had some insight into Olivia's anxiety.

"Sorry we ruined your party," Nick said, stressing *your*.

"Her mother would be ashamed," she said, also stressing *her*. Nick knew what that meant. Olivia was Alison's mother but not his.

"Yeah, I'm guessing she would be ashamed. Ashamed that *her* sister never went out to visit *her* while she was taking care of *her* dying husband. That *her* sister never helped *her* kids while *their* parents were sick." Nick took a breath. "Only here at the end for the pomp and circumstance, to put on a little victory lap in your husband's gawdy mansion."

Aunt Azalea looked like she was about to give him a piece of her mind and Nick was ready for a fight, craving it. Instead, she huffed then turned around. He guessed she probably wasn't used to people standing up to her. After she trotted down the steps, Nick heard the bathroom door creak open.

"That was awesome," Alison giggled.

"C'mon," Nick replied. "Let's get the fuck out of here."

He helped her down the steps and out the door to his car. A few guests indulged them with understanding smiles, as if to say, *Yes, she's allowed this moment of weakness considering the circumstances.* Nick doubted he'd be allowed the same grace. Alison kept a hand over her eyes on the drive downtown to the Sheraton. He was grateful she never threw up on his seat. She didn't need help getting up to her room. Nick went to the bathroom as she flopped on a couch and took out her phone. He could hear her talking.

"I'm telling you I'm fine…yes, g'night…love you."

Nick came out and sat down across from her.

"I s'pose you heard that, did you?" she asked.

"The last bit."

"It was my partner."

"You've never mentioned a…partner before. How long have you guys been together?"

"A couple years."

"Couldn't make it to the funeral?"

"I think you know why."

"Oh c'mon, do you really think people are going to make a big deal of that at this point? And fuck them if they did."

"I guess you've known all along."

"I had my suspicions."

"Mom and dad didn't know."

"I doubt that."

"I was afraid of what they'd think."

"I think they would've been fine with it, honestly."

"Yeah, but you know how they are—were. They'd be fine with it, but they'd be anxious about how they were going to explain it to everyone."

"You mean Aunt Azalea."

Alison laughed. "The idea of disappointing them terrifies me. It's pathetic. I'm almost forty-years old, and I'm still desperate for my parents' approval. And it's not like it even means anything at this point. Dad's gone and mom is just about a vegetable herself. I wish I'd had some of your rebelliousness."

"I'm not so sure about that."

"I was so jealous of you when you were a teenager, playing in a punk band, living your life how you wanted. I wish I could've told mom and dad to shove it a few times like you."

"Funny because I was jealous of you back then. It felt like I was living in your shadow. You were so good at school and sports. You made it look so easy."

"It wasn't easy. It was never easy. Everything they did was out of love, they wanted the best for us, but they pushed, they pushed hard. That's why I had to stay in Toronto. After I finished my degree at UofT I couldn't come home. I needed the space to try and live life on my own terms as best I could."

Alison groaned and peeled herself up off from the chair. She went to the mini fridge and grabbed a bottle of water. After a couple mouthfuls, she picked up the room phone and ordered a pizza from room service.

"Sorry, I should've asked if you wanted anything," she said. "You can have some pizza."

"That's fine."

"What about you and Charlotte? Everything OK there?"

"I got wasted last night and made a scene. Going to need some time before I try and patch things up."

"She seems like a good girl."

"You would know."

They both laughed at that.

There was a knock at the door; the pizza had arrived. Nick realized he hadn't eaten anything substantial all day, just that donut before the funeral and bits and pieces from Aunt Azalea's pretentious charcuterie boards. He and Alison shared slices of pizza that oozed with gooey cheese, just the way he liked it. Her room at the Sheraton had a postcard-worthy view of The Narrows. The blinking light of a small ship bobbed in the night between the steep rocky cliffs of Signal Hill and Fort Amherst, making its way out into the Atlantic. They shared stories of all the things about Fred and Olivia that had drove them crazy over the years. It was the closest he'd ever felt to his sister in his life.

***

Nick parked his car on the street by the address the woman had given him over the phone. Brown brick government housing duplexes dotted the street along both sides. A mother sitting on her stoop watched him from the corner of her eyes while her kids played on the grass. He wondered if she suspected who he was; these little neighbourhoods were likely similar to the outports for gossip. Maybe they were similarly suspicious of outsiders.

As he walked up to the woman's house, he tried to analyze his emotions. Anxiety, excitement, and curiosity competed equally for the forefront of mind. He wasn't sure what he expected or wanted from this meeting. If he were being honest with himself, he'd been fantasizing about this moment since he was a teenager. Sometimes he'd imagine himself confronting his biological parents with righteous anger, demanding how they could abandon their son like that. To let him go hungry then relinquish their rights as parents at the first offer to take him off their hands, like he was some troublesome puppy. Other times, he imagined (hoped) that something would click inside his mind when he met them, some existential puzzle piece would fall into place and fill the formless gap within him. Whether the encounter was good or bad, an ineffable question would finally be answered, and he wouldn't have to lie in bed at night wrestling with emotions that couldn't be put into words.

He knocked on the door and after a brief wait, it opened to reveal a woman who made him think more of an older sister than a mother. She was, after all, only about fifteen years older than him. They both paused to consider each others' faces. Yes, there could be no doubt. She had the same brown eyes and long eyelashes. Despite that, Nick felt no vague sense of familiarity, which he'd suspected might have happened. They smiled timidly until she reached towards him with a hug.

"It's nice to meet you," Pamela said.

"Same," Nick replied.

He followed her into the kitchen where she poured them tea. They discussed the perfunctory details of their lives. She worked at Sobeys in the west end of St. John's as a cashier, somewhere Nick rarely frequented and therefore likely wouldn't have run into her. He told her about his schooling and job at the university, which she was very keen to know more about. After these superficial topics were exhausted, Pam held her tea cup with both hands and leaned back in her chair. Her kitchen was small and simple. On the fridge was a large magnet containing the

Serenity Prayer: "God, grant me the serenity to accept the things I cannot change, courage to change the things I can, and wisdom to know the difference." There were other small religious paraphernalia around the house—the trappings of someone who'd come to Jesus late in life, more specifically through Alcoholics Anonymous. Normally he'd roll his eyes at stuff like that but after everything with Moore and now more recently his Uncle Jim, he began to appreciate the significance of spiritual conviction. And while he was by no means about to become a Born Again Christian, he could see how belief, particularly belief in the absurd, the impossible, had a trickle down effect. If you were willing to believe in life everlasting, then perhaps believing in your own ability to handle the batshit stuff going on in your life wasn't such a leap of faith.

"I suppose you must have a lot of questions," she said. "And I owe you a lot of answers. Where would you like to start?"

"What about my father?" he asked, doing his best not to come across like a detective interrogating a murder suspect.

"His name is Adam Blackwood. Not long after you were born, he left for Alberta, and I haven't heard from him since. You can look him up on Facebook. I thought about messaging him and letting him know that I'd contacted you, but I figured I'd let you make that decision."

Nick nodded and waited for her to continue.

"We were just stupid teenagers," she explained. "When I got pregnant, I dropped out of school and ran away from home. Then, when you were born, and Adam left, I felt in over my head. I started drinking and eventually doing drugs. I don't know why I thought I could take care of a kid."

Nick felt detached from this story, like it was someone else's life. There was no sense of resentment on his part; he knew all too well the urge to turn to drugs and booze when things felt like they were spiralling out of control. What was the point of being angry at this woman?

"Eventually I reached out to my parents for help," she said. "They took care of you a few times while I tried to get my life together, but I never could. And they were never parents of the year themselves. Not that I'm trying to pass off my problems on them. Then there was that incident at school and child services took you away."

She took a sip of tea before she went on.

"To be honest with you, it was a relief. I knew it was the right thing, I just couldn't bring myself to do it before. After that, I hit rock bottom. I felt like such a failure. So, I got into recovery, got a job, and that's been my life ever since, really. I've had some ups and downs since then, but I go to AA meetings regularly and work hard on my sobriety."

Nick smiled. He was genuinely happy for her. It was a common story that could have gone either way. He thought about Phil and some other friends he knew who were transitioning now from Dumb Kids to Adults With Problems.

"What about your parents?" she asked.

Nick filled her in on all of that.

"I'm sorry to hear about that," she said when he was finished. "But they sound like good people. And you turned out pretty good."

"Yeah," he said. "They were good people."

They said their goodbyes shortly after that. She expressed a desire to keep in touch, and Nick genuinely hoped they would. He got in his car and drove towards Bowring Park. It was a lovely, early spring day, a rare occurrence in St. John's. He needed a walk in the fresh air to sort through his thoughts. Pam was right. His parents were good people, and they'd done their best for him. Wasn't that the most you could ask of your parents? They were fucked up people with their own problems who'd made it up as they went along, just like everyone else. So, what did he owe them? He owed them his best.

CHAPTER EIGHT

Nick sat with Agnes Noonan in her living room, sharing tea. This time he made sure to drink it as the story he'd told her was very long and he needed to take a few breaks to soothe his dry throat. He told her everything about the merchant's mansion, the fairy world Cachot Cove, and his battle with Moore. The only thing he left out was the zombie lines with Landphil. She didn't need to know about all that.

Agnes nodded along and when he was done, she sighed. "Yes, I suspected as much."

An understated response.

She stood up to go refill her tea. Nick noticed she was hunched over now and tottered like a woman her age would be expected to. She sat back down and sighed again. "I've felt tired these past few weeks. I guess that has to do with you breaking the spell Mr. Moore had over that house or whatever it was. Some of that magic must have rubbed off on me after all. Now it's just about wore out."

"You told me to stay out of the woods behind the house," Nick said. "What's in there?"

Agnes took her time and drank her tea. "I don't know for sure, but I suspect it must have something to do with the faeries. I've always felt something queer coming from that place and I don't like it."

"I think it's my only chance."

Agnes shrugged. "You may be right."

"If I am, then that'll be the end of Moore's magic." Nick let that hang there for her to connect the dots.

"How old do you think I am?" she asked. "I knows you've tried to guess. Everyone has."

"At least ninety-seven?" Nick ventured.

Agnes smiled. "One-hundred and four." She pointed towards her wall of photographs. "My four children are dead. I even have a dead grandchild. I've had enough life. It's clung to me like a stain. I can't get rid of it. You do whatever you have to do and don't worry about me. It's well past my time, honey."

Nick and Agnes exchanged their goodbyes. He tried to not to think this might be the last he'd see her alive — or what would become of him if he failed. He left and made his way over to the merchant's mansion. There wasn't much use, but he entered the house anyway. Wandering around, it was easy to tell the connection was broken. It was just an ordinary house now, made up of bricks and wood, subject to the same laws of atrophy as the rest of the universe. He sat down on the living room sofa and remembered waking with Charlotte after their fight with Moore. At the time, he'd thought the house had felt like it was less oppressive, but now as he was sitting in this exorcized house, he realized that before the curse was broke, the house had felt thin, as if there was only a thin sheath separating this world and the other world, the supernatural world, the fairy world, whatever it was called. If he had to put it into words, it was like leaning over a cliff, where the wind was so heavy you almost dared to lean all the way over and it would catch you and float you away. Now, he was safely inland. But that was no use to him. He needed that wind to carry him off.

Looking at the living room fireplace, he again admired its artistry. The mantle's marble was masterfully carved into delicate leaves and branches with two nymphs at the top centre reaching towards a little tree. The woods, of course. That's where he needed to go. He knew he was just procrastinating here in the merchant's mansion, hoping some alternative would present itself, and he wouldn't have to venture into the deep, dark woods. But you didn't need to be a folklorist to know that's not how fairy tales went. It was down to him, now. Neither Charlotte, Alison, nor his parents could bail him out.

He walked outside and found the old footpath Moore had taken many times before. A breath parted the thick bramble, disentangling branches to form a hallway like a long set of steepled fingers. And there it was, that thinness, that great wind waiting to float him away. Nick ducked down and entered. The smell of sap and damp moss filled his nostrils. Except for the small crunching of his footsteps over small twigs and leaves, it was deathly quiet. While the birds and other critters had started coming around the mansion, they still left the woods alone. A claw clutched at his shoulder. He yelped and swatted away the branch. When he turned, he could see the way back had now collapsed into a tightly knotted web of branches and twigs, like he was trapped inside a chaotic wicker basket. There was no turning back now so he turned around and continued on the path laid out for him.

The weald couldn't have been bigger than a kid's softball field, but he felt like he'd been walking for at least ten minutes, and there was still no end in sight. He looked up, searching for the sun, and found it obscured by colossal sequoias, stretching high into the sky. The diameters of the trunks must have been thirty feet. Trees normally found in British Columbia and California on the Pacific Coast, not out here in the North Atlantic. That was fine; he'd expected the impossible.

The trail ended and opened into a wide clearing. It was warm now, almost tropical. The cedar and spruce now gave way to a green inferno of wide palm leaves. Nick now felt like he was on the set of a Vietnam movie, wandering haplessly through the jungle, waiting for Charlie to sneak up on him and run him through with a rusty bayonet. He choked back an overwhelming sense of panic. The last time he could remember feeling this lost was when he was five, running around the aisles of the grocery store, screaming for his mom. That's when he heard it. A whisper.

Hellllllp

He closed his eyes and focused on the sound. It drifted towards him, rustling the leaves. He recognized it. It had called out to him before. Heat emanated angrily from the source of the voice, like the Elephant's Foot in Chernobyl. He parted two palm leaves that were bigger than him to reveal a gnarled, black tree bent like an old man's spine. Nick stepped over thick, branching roots, interwoven across the forest floor. Leafless branches stretched from the tree's crown like twisted, arthritic fingers. The bloated trunk was split and held together by iron bands. Nick approached it and held his hands towards the tree, the bark covered with peculiar green and yellow streaks and blotches. The iron bands radiated angry heat. Something was glowing within the tree's slits. When Nick tried to peer through, a centipede crawled out, stretching its drunken antennae. Nick stepped back. The insect fully emerged from the tree. It must have been a foot long. Nick felt something crawl across his feet. He looked down and the roots were teeming with furry spiders, their abdomens fat as kiwis.

You have his mark, a voice from within the tree spoke.

Nick's shoulder burned.

It wasn't a human voice, not quite. Some amalgamation of the wind rustling the leaves and branches in harmony with the clicking of insects came together to speak.

"Are you the one who gave Moore his power?"

An angry laugh shook the forest. *I was deceived. He offered me sanctuary. Even then the world was shrinking. Shrunken by your people. You spread like mould, covering the world with your infection, chopping down the forests, flooding the night with your harsh, incessant glow. Nowhere to hide, nowhere to run, nowhere to grow. No place for roots.*

"He's deceived a lot of people."

I know what he's done. Did you come to mock me?

"I need your help." The spiders sat still in the quiet forest, waiting for how this parlay would play out—ready for attack. Nick continued. "I need passage to his territory."

What's in it for me? an answer came after a long silence.

Nick considered this. "Revenge."

The air in the forest flattened and all Nick could hear was the buzzing of insects. The sound rose and fell hypnotically until they all matched frequency, riding the same wavelength. Nick's eyes fluttered until they finally shut, and he stood in a deep state of meditation, unable to notice the spiders bigger than dinner plates descending from the tree tops onto his head and shoulders, and the five-foot centipedes crawling up his legs. Then a scorpion bigger than a cat attached itself to his back. There was a brief moment of panic as he felt his body become encased in a swarming sarcophagus, but he could feel the planes open and the great wind floated him away.

When Nick opened his eyes, he was standing at the treeline, looking at Cachot Cove, Moore's Cachot Cove. Across the wharf stood Moore's castle. The men and women working stopped and looked up. For the first time since they could remember, clouds obscured the sun. It was puzzling to behold. As Nick walked past the wharf, he saw his father standing amongst the other men. They locked eyes.

"Nick!" his father screamed, shaking his shoulders. "What the hell are you doing back...?"

Nick turned to face his dad and Fred stopped once he saw the yellow glow in his son's eyes. Nick turned away and walked towards the castle.

It was empty. The halls were dusty and full of cobwebs. Tiny flies buzzed around rotten, maggoty food in the dining hall. Nick passed the library and saw that it was no bigger than his high school's. He found Moore slumped over his throne, old, haggard, shriveled. His robes fell loosely around him, revealing an ugly, festering wound where Nick had stabbed him with the railroad spike. When Moore saw Nick enter, he rushed towards him, still some of that old strength within him. But Nick's yellow glowing eyes stopped him short.

"Thamorelle?" he whimpered. "Wait. Listen to me. Don't do this. I'll let your parents go. I'll let everyone go. I can teach you. Show you how to make your own paradise. You don't know what you're throwing away."

Nick opened his mouth and tiny spiders streamed out of him like from a hose attached to a fire hydrant. As they plopped to the floor, they grew wings and enlarged sevenfold. The spiders swarmed around Moore, buzzing with furious intensity. He screamed, flailed his arms and tried to get away, but it was useless. They pinned him to the wall and got to work. Nick's skin crawled watching it unfold.

"Nick!" Moore pleaded. "Stop this, please. This place won't survive without me. Your parents are as good as dead. Think about the li—"

Before Moore could finish his words, the spiders had cocooned him. Nick could only hear muffled cries coming from inside the wriggling mass of webs. The flying spiders then buzzed away and began swirling into a cone that eventually took humanoid form. The squirming mass congealed into a seven-foot tall androgynous figure who looked down upon Nick with high cheekbones and yellow eyes.

"He told you my name," Thamorelle said in a sonorous voice that reminded Nick of David Bowie. "Now you have power over me. This place is yours."

Nick had outsmarted Moore after all. Cachot Cove, the library, eternal life, it was all his. He closed his eyes and before him sat a great typewriter atop an old wooden desk. His fingers drifted over the keys. Their spidery stems struck the paper with a staccato rhythm. When Nick opened his eyes, the old medieval castle had been replaced by a rustic Italian villa with wooden beams and warm creamy walls.

Nick shook his head. "I don't want it. I just want this to be over—to let everyone go."

Thamorelle shrugged. "That's up to you."

Nick closed his eyes again. This time, he saw a modern computer panel with a glowing red "Delete" button in the top right corner.

"What will you do with him?" Nick asked, gesturing towards Moore.

"He'll be a nice decoration," Thamorelle replied.

"What'll happen to everyone I free?" Nick asked.

"You're asking about the after-life," Thamorelle answered. "But that's the ultimate threshold of knowledge, even for someone as ancient as myself. Moore spent several of your lifetimes trying to outthink it, but failed."

"Well, what do you think happens?"

Thamorelle laughed. "I don't think about it at all. It's a very human phenomenon to dwell on death. Compared to me, your time on this planet is a blink of the eye. And the more you increase your lifespans, the more you fret over it. I find it exhausting to be around."

"Where will you go now that you're free? You can

hang around the forest behind the merchant's mansion still if you want."

Thamorelle eyed him caustically. "I'll take my chances elsewhere."

"I don't blame you."

Anguished, suppressed wails came from inside the cocoon, which delighted Thamorelle, but Nick couldn't stand to listen to it.

"Perhaps it's time you said your goodbyes," Thamorelle advised, not looking away from where Moore was glued to the wall.

Thamorelle didn't strike Nick as someone who exchanged handshakes or other pleasantries, so he just turned around and left the castle. Outside, his parents and the rest of Moore's former prisoners stood waiting. They seemed happy but anxious, excited to finally leave but also unsure of what awaited them. But they were ready for it, nonetheless.

Olivia ran to him, tears in her eyes, and hugged him fiercely. He could no longer count on one hand how many times he'd seen her cry now. When she released him, Fred was standing there, waiting. He and Nick took a walk.

"You did it," Fred said, after some time, his eyes fixed on his shoes. He was older now, closer to what he looked like shortly before he'd bought the merchant's mansion, trim like an old coach who could still do laps with the team, just a little grey around his sideburns.

"Probably didn't think you had it in me," Nick said.

Fred stopped and looked out over the bay. The water lay still like a mirror, reflecting the sky's pink and red hues. Split in half, the setting sun sat atop the ocean spilling out like a burst yolk.

"When I was around twelve, I lost my dad," Fred said. "You know this, but I rarely talked about it. Before he died, the last conversation we had was an argument. It was about him not wanting me to be a fisherman. He wanted me to get an education, to become a teacher. So, I did. He was probably right. But it burned me up that I felt like I had to live out my life like he wanted me to. And I only realize now that I tried to do the same with you and your sister. We were hard on you guys. Maybe too hard at times." He looked at Nick who looked back at his father incredulously. "Yeah, maybe more often than not. But the world is a tough, mean place and we wanted you to be ready for it. Myself and your mother, we used to feel frustrated that you didn't take direction like Alison. What I realize now is that we were frustrated because you didn't need it. Scared, really. Scared of not being in control. Life has a way of beating that into you, that need for control. I hope you don't fall into the same trap. You were always ready to meet the world on your terms and find your own path. I wish I'd seen that earlier, instead of fighting you all the time, trying to force you down a familiar path I knew and was more comfortable with. I wish I'd let you lead and followed behind you, seen where your trail took you. Maybe I'll still be able to. Who knows?" Fred looked out over the sunset on the ocean. "At least you still have your mother. Just take it easy on her, OK?" Fred turned and hugged Nick tightly. "Time to let go," he said.

Nick closed his eyes and saw the flashing button. He felt the desperate need to cling to this moment. He opened his eyes again and saw his father watching him. Fred was old now, more like how Nick remembered, shortly before he got sick. He looked tired, ready to move on. Nicked realized this was the last he was going to see him in the flesh—or whatever the hell this all is. After that, it was going to be only memory. But that was OK, this was how he wanted to remember his dad. It was time. Nick closed his eyes again and approached the red button. When he pressed it, he felt a woosh followed by a pop. He opened his eyes and saw a grey, drab sky between shrubs and skinny branches. He was lying on the ground and to his right, he could see the merchant's mansion. To his left, he could see where the cliffs of Cachot Cove dropped off into the ocean. The passageway was sealed now, and the world here was solid through and through. He could feel it.

"I love you, dad," he whispered.

A cold wind off the sea rustled the branches, sending a chill up Nick's back. It crossed the harbour all the way to the other side of Cachot Cove, where Agnes Noonan sat in her living room chair, looking out over the bay. Ready for rest, she closed her eyes and let go of life.

* * *

Nick poured a teaspoon of creamer into his coffee and watched it swirl around his mug in a tiny vortex. He filled another mug of coffee with milk and sugar and handed it to Charlotte.

"Happy birthday," she said and fetched a card from her purse. It was pretty generic—just an image of a cake with some candles. Inside was a $20 gift card for Chapters. It was both thoughtful and impersonal. It said: *I care about you but I'm not about to take you back so easily.*

They sat at the small table of their apartment, although Nick supposed it was technically his apartment now. Charlotte had moved all her stuff out not too long after his father's death. Aside from the odd text, this was the first time they'd sat down to talk in person since then.

It was a warm August afternoon, but he felt moody and tired. In the three months since his father's death, he'd wake up some days totally lethargic despite sleeping eight hours or more. Alison reported feeling the same way. However, unlike during the time when Fred was sick, Nick didn't feel that cocktail of melancholia, anxiety, dread, and the myriad other twisted thoughts and emotions that had swirled around him in that long, exhausting year. Now, it was simply sadness. Grief, he supposed it was. Like Uncle Jim had said, grief was that old drunk that came knocking unexpectedly and you couldn't just rush him out. So, Nick took his uncle's advice, and allowed himself to sit with grief and hear it out. And it was oddly comforting to allow himself to feel that, to feel the sadness work its way through him, like an unclogged stream flowing the polluted water out.

"How's therapy going?" she asked.

"Great," Nick answered. After he'd sold the merchant's mansion, settled up with Alison, and set aside money for helping his mom, he still had about $200,000 in the bank, something he wasn't familiar with. He hired a consultant to help him invest about $150,000 in stocks. The rest he used towards stuff like counselling, as well as massage therapy to try and get the kinks out of his shoulder, but something told Nick that was a wound he'd carry for the rest of his life. He also registered for an online copywriting course that was starting in the fall.

"Is it grief counselling?" Charlotte asked.

"No," Nick answered. "We haven't even gotten to that at all. We're talking about my past and the stuff with my biological parents."

"I'm happy for you," she said.

"A lot about letting go of anger, learning how to process those feelings instead of burying them down and letting them fester." Nick took a sip of coffee before continuing. "It's definitely helped me realize some of the unhealthy patterns I was continuing in my life. I thought that after I'd stopped partying so much and got back to school, that I'd figured my life out and everything was fine, but that wasn't true. I still kept everyone at an arm's length, my family, friends, and especially you. That night I came home wasted after dad died, and said all that nasty shit, you were right when you told me that all the shit that's happened to me wasn't my fault but was still my responsibility."

"Is that why you asked me to come here?"

Nick paused to take another sip of coffee, but his mug was empty. "Yeah, mostly to apologize. Not just for that night when I came home fucked up and said all that awful stuff, but also how I treated you in our relationship in general. I wish I'd let you in, told you about the stuff about my biological parents earlier. Just…I don't know…" Nick had rehearsed this conversation a number of times but was now at a loss for words. Now he wished he'd made a checklist of things he'd wanted to say like he did before a session with his therapist. *Stop trying to be clever, just say it*, he told himself. "I took you for granted. I saw you as a source of comfort instead of a partner in a relationship who I needed to invest in. And that I loved you. I still love you. I didn't say that enough."

"Thanks," she said, wiping away some tears. "I love you too."

Nick felt like he was going to faint after finally getting all that out. He certainly didn't want to push his luck any further. "I have to go visit mom. Do you want to get together again soon?"

"Yeah, that'd be nice," she said.

He walked her out of the apartment building, and they hugged before she left and got into her car. Nick got into his and drove towards CBS where he'd gotten his mom a small apartment. She'd made a steady recovery in the months after he'd released Moore's hold on her. Her speech was still slurred, and her vision wasn't good enough to drive, but she could live independently. Aside from visiting her almost every day, he drove her to her physio and speech therapy appointments.

Inside, she was cooking stir fry. Nick watched her unsteady hand clumsily stir the spatula with a shaky grip.

"Here, mom," he said, "let me help you."

She swatted him away with her other hand. "No," she said. Stubborn as ever.

They sat down together at the table and watched *Jeopardy* as they ate. If his dad were here, he'd never allow the television to be on during supper, but Nick guessed this was a rule his mom no longer agreed with. He did, however, remember to take off his hat. Uncle Jim had been right about death allowing you to remember loved ones as you wanted. You can choose what to remember and what to forget. Nick was beginning to see that forgetting was a powerful tool. On the surface, remembrance meant overcoming forgetfulness. Instead, paradoxically, forgetting was the heart of memory. The brain strengthened whatever memories we repeated over our lives. That's why Fred could remember playing hockey as a kid but not what he'd ate for breakfast. Those neural pathways had been re-threaded so many times over his lifetime. Forgetting meant choice. Nick could choose what memories he wanted to replay over and over in his mind of his father, mother, sister, whoever. He chose to strengthen the memories of when his parents let him and his band practice in their basement despite having zero appreciation for the racket they made; of when his parents surprised him with a new Fender Strat on his first day of high school; of when his dad had taught him to ride a bike without training wheels. When he stretched his mind, the earliest memory he had of Fred was when they were at a swimming pool, and Nick was afraid to jump in. He could see his dad stretching his arms out, his forearms roped with veiny muscles. Nick could vividly remember telling himself, *Those arms are strong, he can catch me.* So, he jumped. Did he actually think that as a child at the time? Maybe, maybe not. Memory had a way of imposing the present upon the past with each fresh recollection. But that was how Nick chose to remember it, nonetheless.

As for his mother, it seemed like she'd forgotten her time as Moore's prisoner. Whether this was a conscious choice, Nick wasn't sure. At this point of the day, she was tired and could only really manage single word sentences.

And Nick had no interest in pushing the issue. He was happy to sit with her, watch *Jeopardy*, and share their silence.

Just then Olivia looked up into the corner of the room and her brow hardened. A small spider had formed a web there. She grabbed a copy of *The Telegram* and rolled it up. Extending her arm like Serena Williams performing an overhand serve, she struck the spider mercilessly. She looked at Nick and something flashed across her face, like she'd just remembered something. From her purse, she retrieved an envelope and handed it to Nick.

"'appy bir'day," she whispered.

Jeopardy soon ended and Nick gave his mom a goodbye hug. She was frail to hold, but he could feel the strength in her embrace. In the car, he opened his birthday card. He pushed aside a $50 bill to read the nice Hallmarky message about the love between a parent and their child. Normally he'd find that kind of stuff schmaltzy, but he thought it was sweet, nonetheless. He also rolled his eyes at the fact his mother felt the need to give him $50 despite the sale of the merchant's mansion. At the bottom of the card, he saw that his mother had signed it. It just said "Love, mom." Normally, she'd have long messages about the past and future, hopes and dreams, written with flowing script. It made him sad to see her once gorgeous handwriting reduced to a childlike scrawl. But he recognized that it must have meant a lot to his mother to be able to sign it despite her penmanship.

He saw also that something seemed to have been rubbed out beside "mom." Like she'd made a mistake and tried to erase it. Squinting, he could pick out the pen's indentations. It had said: "& dad."

AFTERWORD

In 2018, when I published my first novel, *After Dark Vapours*, I dedicated it to my dad. Writing a novel requires a lot of hard work, dedication, and perseverance; it's often boring, frustrating, and the end can seem nowhere in sight. I wouldn't have been able to finish that book, or the two I've written since, without the lessons dad taught me growing up about, what he called, "stick-to-it-ness."

But I wouldn't have been a writer in the first place if it weren't for my mom. For bedtime stories she used to read me Edgar Allen Poe; her favourite was "The Cask of Amontillado"—she even had it committed to memory. Mom was able to foster in me a love for reading because she was never a snob about what I read. If I wanted RL Stine, she got me Goosebumps. If I wanted Spider-Man and Batman, she brought me to Downtown Comics every BOGO Wednesday. She was like those cliché drug dealers in after-school movies, who knew that if they could just get you hooked on the soft stuff, then it was a gateway to the harder shit. So RL Stine became Tolkien who became Stephen King who became HP Lovecraft then we're right back to Poe before taking a hard turn to Ernest Hemingway and James Joyce. Now I couldn't kick the habit even if I wanted to.

Mom went through hell after dad was diagnosed with Alzheimer's. So did my sister and I. But mom especially. Caring for someone with dementia takes a toll the extent of which can't be put into discursive language, which is why we have metaphor, and hopefully I was able to translate some of that in this book. So, while this book is primarily dedicated to my mom, I'd also like to dedicate it to anyone reading this who has also had to care for someone diagnosed with dementia. I hope you feel some of your experiences, thoughts, and emotions were represented here and perhaps you got to feel the same kind of catharsis I had writing it.

DARK STORIES FROM ENGEN BOOKS

THE HOWL BECONS

Growing up without his father, Tyler had no way of knowing the horrible secret that has plagued his family for generations. To free himself and find the cure, he will have to look beyond himself and into his dark history.

"A very ambitious novel... the horrors of everyday life can be worse than anything in fiction. The idea of using werewolves as a metaphor – to me this pushes the book a bit above much of what is out there... Brad [Dunne] is a very good writer and obviously has a deep background."
— Andrew Peacock

WESTON'S WAR

Something evil grows in the heart of Colorado. Bill Weston was a man of the West. He knew it – its land, its people, its stories. It was where he plied his trade, hunting men for money. His life wasn't easy, but it was predictable. That all changed when he captured Faraway Sue and he was led on a trip through the Colorado forests

"Take a little Zane Grey. Add a little Penny Dreadful. Read with Sam Elliot's voice. Discover Jon Dobbin's masterful The Starving."
— Darrell Power,
Great Big Sea

ABOUT THE AUTHOR

Brad Dunne is a freelance writer and editor from St. John's, Newfoundland. He began his writing career as an intern at *The Walrus* magazine and has published journalism and essays in publications such as *Maisonneuve*, *The Canadian Encyclopedia*, and *Herizons*. His short fiction has been featured in *In/Words*, *Acta Victoriana*, *The From the Rock Series*, *Terror Nova*, and, *The Cuffer Anthology*.

In October 2018 he released his first novel, *After Dark Vapours*. It was followed in September 2020 by *The Gut*. *The Merchant's Mansion* is his third novel.

He maintains a blog at braddunne.ca. He's also active on twitter (@braddunne1796) and instagram (@yoloflaherty).